# Heir Apparent

Tyree Campbell

**Heir Apparent
by Tyree Campbell**

All rights reserved. No part of this book may be reproduced or transmitted in any form or by any means, electronic or mechanical, including photocopying or recording or by any information storage and retrieval systems, without expressed written consent of the author and/or artists.

*Heir Apparent* is a work of fiction. Names, characters, places, and incidents are products of the author's imagination. Any resemblance to actual events or persons, living or dead, is entirely coincidental.

Story copyright owned by Tyree Campbell
Cover illustration "Tourist Trap" by Laura Givens
Cover design by Laura Givens

First Printing, November 2023

Hiraeth Publishing
P.O. Box 1248
Tularosa, NM 88352
e-mail: hiraethsubs@yahoo.com

Visit www.hiraethsffh.com for online science fiction, fantasy, horror, scifaiku, and more. Stop by our online bookstore for novels, magazines, anthologies, and collections. **Support the small, independent press...and your First Amendment rights.**

## Also by Tyree Campbell

**Nyx Series (Novels):**
*Nyx: Malache*
*Nyx: Mystere*
*Nyx: The Protectors*
*Nyx: Pangaea*
*Nyx: The Redoubt*

**Yoelin Thibbony Rescues (Novels)**
*The Butterfly and the Sea Dragon* *
*The Moth and the Flame* *
*The Thursday Child**
*Avatar*

**Lark Series (Novels)**
*The Desert Lark*
*The Iphajean Lark*
*The Justice Lark*
*The Traffic Lark*
*The Illusion Lark*

**Novels:**
*The Adventures of Colo Collins &
Tama Toledo in Space and Time*
*The Adventures of Colo Collins &
Tama Toledo in Love and in Trouble*
*Aoife's Kiss*
*The Breathless Stars*
*The Dice of God*
*The Dog at the Foot of the Bed*
*The Dog at War*
*The Gifted*
*Heir Apparent*
*Indigo*

*Iuliae: Past Tense*
*The Quinx Effect*
*Starwinders: Nohana's Heart*
*Starwinders: Nohana's Triangles*
*Thuvia, Maid of Earth*
*A Wolf to Guard the Door*
*The Woman from the Institute*

**Superheroine Novellas:**
*Bombay Sapphire 1* \*\*
*Bombay Sapphire 2* \*\*
*Bombay Sapphire 3* \*\*
*Bombay Sapphire 4* \*\*
*Oliva Sudden 1*
*Peridot 1*
*Peridot 2*
*Peridot 3*
*Peridot 4*
*Voyeuse 1*
*Voyeuse 2*
*Voyeuse 3*

**Collections:**
*AbracaDrabble*
*Drink Before the War*
*A Nice Girl Like You*
(published by Khimairal, Inc)
*Quantum Women* \*

**Novellas:**
*Becoming Jade*
*Cloudburst*
*Future Tense*
*The Girl on the Dump*
*The Martian Women*
*Sabit the Sumerian*
*Sarrow*

**Poetry Collections**
*A Danger to Self and Others*

**SF for Younger Readers**

*Pyra and the Tektites 1*
*Pyra (graphic novel) 1*
*Pyra and the Tektites 2*
*Pyra (graphic novel) 2*
*Pyra and the Tektites 3*
*Pyra and the Tektites 4*
*Pyra and the Tektites 5*
*Pyra and the Tektites 6*


\* published by Nomadic Delirium Press

\*\* published by Pro Se Press

All titles are available from the Shop at
www.hiraethsffh.com

# Prologue

The boundaries of the satrapy of Wanderby had been vague since the three brothers and their families and cohorts had settled onto Byzneen, the second largest continent of Faedra, four centuries earlier. Initially, unoccupied farmland had attracted them, but it was the mineral wealth in the range of low mountains that arced through their vast claimstake that had induced them to settle permanently. Ores of platinum, tungsten, and rare-earths made the brothers wealthy within a generation. There was no fratricidal bickering, for there was more than enough to go around. "We can live like kings," declared Esa, the youngest of the three brothers, and the ambitious statement sang to them. "Uneasy lies the crown," Paleo, the eldest, reminded them (though he was drunk at the time). "Let's be dukes." And with the agreement of Esa and Lasco, the rank was settled.

It was soon reasoned out that dukes, like kings, ought to reside in castles. The stone that was being quarried from the open mines, and abundant forests on the holding, provided more than sufficient material to build three castles. The hired architects had been compelled to study the ancient structures, but managed to follow those designs...somewhat. Each castle was laid out in a square, with a central courtyard, walls to three levels high, battlements, corner towers, a bailey, and a keep. This last was in reality the domicile, where the duke and his family resided on the upper two levels, and the servants and staff lived and worked on the lowest. A dungeon and a moat were thought unnecessary, but a cellar was included perforce as the walls required a foundation below ground.

The entire claimstake was named Wanderby for no better reason than that it sounded good. Divided more or less equally into three holdings, the mineral riches as well, each holding added basic necessities—including an agricultural village, populated to tend the farms; hedgerows of broken stone to delineate boundaries as well as smaller farm holdings; grazing land; and fruit and nut groves.  Each village knew at least one smokehouse, a tannery, a cannery, a tavern, and structures in which textiles were produced and foodstuffs were preserved.

Despite a few squabbles of short duration, life for everyone was tranquil, and even idyllic, for everyone had enough, or more than enough.  Trade exported ores and imported the technologies that eased overall living. Interpersonal violence, though not unheard-of, was minimized due to the structure of the extended family, for it was thought that proper upbringing produced cooperative citizens.  The population itself reached a point where it was stable, for some went off to other lands on Faedra, or departed for the stars, and the birthrate was sufficient to fill in the gaps.

At length each ducal family found it necessary to continue the legacy.  As in ancient times, primogeniture was the rule, and it was agreed among the three brothers that the eldest male issue was first in line to their respective thrones, and that if there were no male issue, then the eldest female succeeded to the throne.  That there might be no issue at all was not considered, for dukes, being dukes, tended to stray now and then, while the duchesses, keeping their counsel, wisely turned a blind eye, especially as dukes were faithful to them in their own way.  (A century later, one of the successor dukes was known as Portico the Bastard. A quiet sort, he enjoyed oil painting, and was rather good at it).  As in ancient times, so in the contemporary.

Until the ores played out.

Economic stagnation followed.  Not that life became worse; far from it, for wealth more than sufficient to maintain the standard of living had been put aside, and interstellar commerce was active enough to support that standard. There was, in short, no need for greed to supplant the lifeways.

No need, but in time there arose the desire...

# 001: Dialogues

For the better part of two hours the young woman had not spoken, and March was beginning to wonder whether she had spent so much time alone on this remote world that she had forgotten how to speak at all. Still, her gray eyes never wavered from his face, as if she expected to see at any moment answers appear there to her unspoken questions. He had none to give her. Riding the beam of a distress signal—the moral requirement of any space traveler—he had landed here on Calla Cried to assist if possible. But he had found no one in need of aid. If it was the young woman seated on the other side of the campfire he had built, she had yet to broach her request.

March had been on his way to Luxuria, a malchristening if ever there were one. Mining and smelting and exporting were the only activities on the dry desert world, and he'd had the notion of assisting, uninvited, in the export business. A shipment of iridium ingots was due to depart in two days local time, and he meant for it to be aboard his *Bluebolt* a couple hours before its scheduled departure. Already he had two potential buyers for it. But he was running out of time.

Low flames cast the young woman's oval face in orange and shadows. In the twilight earlier March had thought her short, roughly-chopped hair to be the carroty-coppery color of the true redhead; the washes of freckles on her face and pale bare arms strongly hinted at this. But in the flickering light, the hair appeared to be shades of gold, darker where the shadows struck it. Attired in a light-colored top and khaki shorts that almost reached her knees, she had some height to her, almost as much as March's meter-ninety with the aid of the scuffed brown boots she was wearing. Not a pretty face greeted him—her jaw was too strong for beauty, and her straight thin nose had been broken at least once—but he had the impression that hers was a determined and willful expression. Though unarmed, as far as he could tell, she was no one to be trifled with.

More minutes passed, and the flames slowly withered. March tossed a couple more short branches into the shallow pit, the impacts sending a little shower of sparks up toward the darkening sky. For a few moments he watched while the wood ignited. When he looked up from the fire again, she was gone.

In moving, as in speaking, she had not made a sound.

March scanned the woods beyond and the gently rolling plains behind him where his *Bluebolt* rested, and saw no movement, not even the sway of grass in a breeze. The deep twilight might have obscured her, but in any event she was no longer sitting across the fire from him. Her disappearance effectively ended his obligatory rescue mission, for the sensors of Myrrha, his spaceskip's computer as well as his companion, had detected no other intelligent life forms on the planet.

March extinguished most of the fire by peeing on it, and doused the rest from his canteen, before setting out for his 'skip some fifty meters away. Small nocturnal creatures scurried through the calf-high grass and out of his way as he passed over a hillock and around a copse of white-barked trees. Reaching the 'skip's ramp, he turned back for one last look, then ascended up to the hatch. Once aboard, he tokked his Palmetto.

"Myrrha, retract ramp and seal—"

"I'm right here," she said, behind him, having come up from aft.

Startled, he turned back to her. Though she was prone to minor alterations of her hard-light appearance at whim, Myrrha was still a woman in green, who presented herself as in her mid-twenties, or ten years March's junior. Short, myrtle green hair and lips, serpentine eyes, and pale green skin completed her general characteristics.

Aside from them, she looked perfectly human, and his equal in height, and at the moment, like him, she was wearing a gray outsuit and black boots.

"I thought you would be resting inside the 'skipcomp," he said. As he turned to make his way forward to the bridge, she clutched at his elbow, stopping him.

Myrrha had come into existence as the result of an off-hand remark to the 'skipcomp to grow a personality. Two days after that remark, the woman Myrrha had appeared on the bridge, an act that had left March breathless until his ribs ached. The woman and the 'skipcomp were identical in knowledge and intelligence, and continuously self-updated. Unlike the 'skipcomp, however, the woman had aspirations of intimacy.

"I was hoping that this time I would finally do my resting with you," she said, the hint heavy, as she led him aft to a guest stateroom. At the door, she knocked twice. "We're coming in," she called, and slid it open.

Dismayed, March understood immediately upon seeing the interior. "Oh, she didn't."

But the young woman from the campfire did, and got up from the berth as they entered.

Words almost failed him, but he managed a, "Are you talking yet?" almost rudely. A sharp elbow from Myrrha elicited his perfunctory apology.

The young woman just looked at him. Whether she saw him as an insect or a human did not show in her expression. In the light from the overhead panels he saw that she was indeed a pale-skinned, freckled redhead. Now for a name to go with the person.

"Newcombe March," he said, as he had at their initial encounter. He did not offer his hand. "Myrrha here allowed you aboard, and I trust her character judgment. But I'll have your name, and the reason you sent the distress signal, and the reason you're here, or I'll have you off my ship. Your call."

She lowered her gaze to the deck at her feet, and sat back down. When at last she met his eyes again, her expression held the serenity and authority of a vast tranquil ocean. "I am Hoya Catalina Palologa," she declared, in the tone of a formal announcement. March thought it should have been accompanied by a fanfare of trumpets. But he also recognized the name.

"There is already one of those," he said, with just a touch of annoyance. "She has been invested as Princess of Islinglas, first in line to one of the three thrones of Wanderby—"

"But I am the true heir," Hoya cut in, fire in her eyes and ice now in her tone.

"Heiress," Myrrha corrected.

March made a little motion with his hand, a caution for her not to interfere. As a result of the minor distraction, he missed the obvious question. Instead, he asked, "Even if this is true, why did you send the distress signal? Your politics are surely none of my affair."

"I had no way of knowing who would respond," she replied evenly. "My first task was to get off the world on which I had been marooned."

"Marooned by whom?" he asked. "And for how long?"

"By the order of Snarrel Goodling, who is—"

"Who is the majordomo for the Palologa Family," said March. "I know who he is. We have had...dealings. Why would he have you marooned on an island on a remote world?"

The possible princess shook her head. "If you would be kind enough to drop me off on Layby, I shall find my way from there. If I might have from you something to eat? I exhausted my food supply two days ago."

"I'll bring rolls and butter and cheese," said Myrrha, and hurried off.

"I did ask you how long," March reminded her, frowning deeply. If he understood her correctly, she was meant to die on Calla Cried.

"I did not count the days. Perhaps six standard months."

"And the distress signal?"

"It took me that long to construct a generator."

That stunned him. "Out of what?"

"What was left of my Palmetto. The majordomo was unaware that I had concealed the pieces on my person when I was taken from my dungeon cell." She flashed an impatient look. "Is this interrogation over? Food was mentioned, was it not?"

"What's on Layby?" March asked calmly, just as Myrrha returned with a loaded tray.

"I have what is called a *pied à terre* there. And that is the last question I will answer."

While she ate, Myrrha drew him aside and out of hearing range. "The parents of Hoya Catalina stood beside her at the investment ceremony," she whispered. "They raised no objection."

March swore softly at the answer to the question he should have asked. "I missed that, didn't I?" He glanced over his shoulder at Hoya, who was chewing absently, her gaze fixed on the bulkhead before her. "So she's a fake."

"A hasty conclusion reached without substantiation. We should try to learn more."

He shook his head emphatically. "The iridium won't wait."

"There is another and perhaps better possibility of acquiring it," Myrrha told him. "If I can confirm this, will you help her?"

"She doesn't sound as if she wants my help, and in any case I don't know what I could do for her." He resolved himself. "No, set us on a course for Layby, and enTrack."

"Aye, Captain."

For a moment he glared at her, irritated by the stiff formality of her response—a deviation from her customary flippant, *We're gone.* "Myrrha, why are you so interested in this?"

Myrrha turned back toward Hoya. "Because I don't think she is a fake."

\*   \*   \*

The aroma of fragrant incense permeated the small but official room in which sat the majordomo of the satrapy known as Palologa. Rotund and balding, he concealed these negative physical characteristics under a loose gown of floral-print silk and an expert's combover of his fringe of jet-black hair. Despite the attire, he was in no way effeminate. A cruel slash of a mouth and a pair of piercing black eyes on his otherwise bland round face attested to his true nature.

His name was Snarrel Goodling, and he had dominated the Palologa household for more than two decades, ruling it without appearing to do so. Up to a point, much had gone well for him. But ten years earlier the direction of his aims had taken a sharp turn. At that time, the Palologa Family had finally accepted the fact that their thirteen-year-old daughter was to be their sole heir, as Olena Palologa had become barren after two miscarriages—both male, and superior in position to their young daughter. Supervised by Goodling, the girl's training and preparation for her royal duties were begun.

Goodling contemplated this as he sat on a cushioned chair with arms of polished dark wood and a high back, all contoured to his shape to minimize the overall appearance of it. Below him stood the trusted and trusting minion Satrin Hommer, attired in brown tights in a harlequin style and a cap from which dangled a small bell. One slippered foot rested on the lowest of three red-carpeted steps that led up to Goodling's chair while he awaited the majordomo's response to the report he had just presented. Presently Goodling's bleak black eyes regained their focus, and he looked down.

"The lack of life signs does not signify that she is dead," he said, his tone grave and uninflected.

"No, sire, but the island on which she was deposited was well-scanned." He pursed his thick lips, thinking. "Perhaps she was eaten."

"By what?"

Hommer had no answer.

"Have an eyes-on search of the island conducted," ordered Goodling. "Every hectare. Every square meter. A thousand thalers to whoever finds the body or what remains of it. I must be certain before I proceed." *Proceed with the next phase*, he finished silently. "And Hommer…"

"Sire?"

"See to this personally. I hold you responsible."

A desultory wave of his hand dismissed the minion. Hommer blanched as he backed out of the room.

"I must be certain," whispered Goodling, before returning to his contemplations. Timing was always a concern when planning and carrying out an intricate strategy—a long game, as it was called. Crucial moments awaited him in the near future. It was time to remind Clewthe Neerdawell, majordomo of the Lascora Family, of the terms of their agreement.

\* \* \*

From the balcony the young woman who was called Catalina stood gazing down into the courtyard, where her parents were engaged in croquet with two of her older cousins. Invited to participate in the match, she had declined with as much graciousness as she could muster. Although her parents were disappointed—they had invited the cousins, both males, to present themselves as potential suitors—they continued with the match, determined to maintain appearances and good relations. A marriage between her and either cousin would cement the union of two-thirds of the Houses of Wanderby, thereby making it the strongest political and economic entity on the world of Faedra. If she proved willing to accept both suitors, the three thrones of Wanderby would complete the union of the Houses. She, however, had no intention of marrying either of them, and certainly not both, for such a marriage would reduce her position, while her husband(s) actually ruled the thrones.

Catalina shook her head, sending cascades of long tangerine hair over one shoulder and then the other. No, she would be told whom to marry, but not by her parents. Somewhere on Faedra surely there resided her intended; she would be told.

One of the cousins glanced up. Alexor, she thought, as he had the lighter brown hair. A wave from him beckoned her down. She declined this, but waved back—her parents were watching, and she deemed it best to assuage in some small way the petty embarrassment her refusal to participate had brought them. Alexor, like his darker-haired cousin, was by no means uncomely, although there was the little matter of the fungus that continued to grow between his toes despite the best medical efforts to treat it. Recently, she had heard, he had taken to buffing it with pumice.

Catalina cast her gaze further out, and presently a tear formed in her left eye. It blurred her vision, but she let it remain, unable to fathom why it had come to be. But Kamie Isaora, who was standing near the courtyard entrance, was waving up to her, as she had three days earlier and on several occasions prior to that. Kamie, cousin to Pathor, the fourth participant at croquet and heir of the Isaora Family. But there was something about Kamie that drew the young woman to her. Was it physical attraction? She had heard of such relationships, but never considered them. Familiarity, perhaps; she felt that was more likely, but in what way? She knew they had met, but the when and where eluded her. An inexplicable depression set in; she waved back, and went inside.

# 002: Negotiations

Directly down the short hallway to her room went Catalina, one eye still wet, the vision in it blurry. She wished to know the cause of the tears, but some innate fear warned her not to inquire too closely into the matter. Of a certainty she had met and knew Kamie Isaora. When, when? She flopped onto a stuffed chair, long legs akimbo, forearms about to slip from the arms of the chair. Answers refused to reveal themselves. And why had the questions now taken form? She had seen Kamie on several occasions without so much as a molecule of water leaking from her eyes. So why now? Perhaps it was connected in some way to either Pathor Isaura or Alexor Lascora and their visit to be presented. She had seen both cousins on many previous occasions as well, but never...

Catalina thought back. No, never had she seen either or both cousins in connection with Kamie. So what did it mean?

She made a little sound of irritation that echoed softly in the room despite the heavy blue curtains that hung over her window. An unfamiliar feeling wafted into her: that she was about to be caught snooping in someone else's closet, to see what sort of clothes they wore. Already she had been caught once, amidst her mother's finery—so many years ago that now it was but a child's vague recollection. On that occasion the only consequence had been a tolerant smile. This time...a spidery *frisson* of fear began to work its way up her spine, ending only when she ceased all thought of Kamie Isaora.

\* \* \*

"We should have arrived by now," complained March, as he stared at the Videx. Only the matte black of null-space was visible, indicating that the *Bluebolt* was enTracked. But the 'skip should have deTracked before this, and he ought to have been looking at the verdant surface of Layby. It was inconceivable that Myrrha, the 'skip's computer and hard-light companion to March, had made an astrogational miscalculation.

March turned to her; she met his gaze evenly. He folded his arms across his chest and waited, the "Well?" implicit.

"The iridium ingots will be stored in a warehouse on Knuth for ten days," she told him. "They will only be under remote surveillance because no one save the buyer will know of them."

"That's not what I want to know," said March.

Myrrha's lips tightened. "You should help her."

"We haven't budged a stinking millimeter from Calla Cried, have we?"

She lowered her eyes and shook her head. "March," she said softly, not quite looking at him, "In my human form, I am your companion, your protector, and your lover. This you know. This is who I am pleased to be. But I am also your advisor. As the computer, I am obligated to obey your orders. At the moment, my human role as advisor and my computer role as astrogational director are in conflict. While this will not cause me temporarily to crash, it needs to be resolved."

"Resolved by helping Hoya," March sighed.

"That would be one way, yes," Myrrha conceded. "The preferred way."

"You're that certain she is not a fake."

She hedged. "Certainty is a strong word."

March considered briefly. "Ten days?"

"And the acquisition of the ingots will be easier than the one you had planned."

Again he pondered the matter. "I think we still proceed to Layby," he said at last. "A meal and some drinks, and rest. And a talk with Hoya about what can be done, if anything."

"I agree," said Myrrha. "And we're gone."

Hoya was waiting for him in the galley. "I wanted to heat some coffee, but I was afraid of touching anything," she said, backing away as he entered.

March poured a mug for each of them and placed them in the warmer. She watched while he set the timer for one minute, and pushed the Start button. "It's fairly straightforward," he said.

A tiny smile tickled the corners of her mouth. "I thought it might be. And thank you."

He shrugged, and leaned back against the counter, waiting. "It was just a button push."

"I meant, for taking me to Layby."

For a few seconds he hesitated. "We're not just taking you to Layby, Your Highness."

Hoya winced. "Don't," she said. "Don't make fun of me. I *am* the Princess of Islinglas. That *is* my official title."

"Myrrha believes you," he replied. "And I'm trying to." The warmer *bing*ed. He wondered whether the timing was auspicious as he removed the mugs. "Very well: Hoya. I would like to speak with you regarding your difficulties. Perhaps there is something that can be done about them."

Gingerly Hoya sipped from her mug. She seemed to find the two-day-old coffee palatable. "This is good. Newcombe—"

"Please. Just March."

She nodded. "I'm not sure there is anything you can do."

That, thought March, was a slight change of heart. He had anticipated derision upon broaching his offer of assistance. Now there was only a dubious approval. Unfortunately, it matched his own mood: he was uncertain that he could help. But he had more or less promised Myrrha.

"Let's find out what needs to be done," he told her. "You said you had a place to stay on Layby. We can talk there."

Hoya almost laughed. "The cottage probably needs dusting."

"I'll bring rags," said March, and this time she did laugh.

\*  \*  \*

Although his official title was Duke of Palologa, Justinio Palologa was reluctant to put on airs, except at formal functions, which he held to a minimum. Not for him or his wife Olena were lavish displays of elegant robes and bejeweled crowns. They felt themselves simple people caught up in their position. Nominally they held almost unlimited power, but like their predecessors they almost never exercised even a small amount of that. Their chief advisor and majordomo, Snarrel Goodling, who had also served Justinio's father, gave the Family direction, with Justinio's permission or, more often, acquiescence. Justinio abhorred trifles. As long as the Palologa Family holding in Wanderby operated smoothly, he was content.

But Justinio and Olena were approaching an age when it was well to consider the succession. Preparations had already been made, and training had been completed. At Goodling's advice, Hoya Catalina had been sent off at the age of nine to a finishing school for the elite, and had returned just in time for her investment at thirteen. Now, a decade later, she patiently awaited her moment to arrive. Not for a few more years, Justinio thought wryly, considering the matter as he stood on the balcony outside the royal bedroom. The midday sun shone brightly above, and he and Olena still had moments to bask in that light. But was it his imagination, or had the majordomo grown surly of late? Not himself given to mood swings, Justinio had no understanding of them in others. But as long as Goodling did his job...

A light touch at his bare arm aroused him. "You are pensive, my liege," said the Duchess. "Come back to bed."

"It is the middle of the day," he pointed out, patting her hand.

"So it is." Long locks of auburn hair and wisps of gray covered her breast and hung over her pale blue sleeping gown. She parted tresses and flung them back over her shoulder, the invitation to him implicit. "When did that ever stop us?" she asked, the hint of a smile on her lips. "Have we grown so old, my liege?"

Again he patted her hand, as he gazed out upon the courtyard. "Not yet," he replied, in the soft voice of their younger days.

"But you have been thinking. Are you perturbed?"

Justinio hesitated. "Nooo... I was merely recalling the role of the majordomo in history. In the beginning, he managed the king's household. A century or so later, the position had evolved to the point where the king was a mere impotent figurehead and the real authority and power rested with the majordomo."

"You are thinking of the Frankish kingdoms, my liege," she said, moving to stand beside him and look out over the courtyard. "Of Pepin the Short. But that was two millennia ago and more. Matters are now different."

He laughed without humor. "I am not so certain."

She frowned. "Do you suspect Snarrel? But of what?"

"No, nothing like that." He shrugged. "Perhaps it is that I feel ill at ease, and without cause."

She took his hand and led him back inside. "I believe I can help with that," she told him.

\* \* \*

The echoes of footsteps always infested the empty hallways of Palologa House. As Snarrel Goodling trod the glistening marble floors he could scarcely hear his own. Sometimes he wondered whether they were the echoes of the haunted—he had by his orders dispatched quite a few people into the next life. He shuddered, passing through the echoes. Had it been appropriate, he would have summoned Catalina to his office and quarters. But appearances, for now, had to be maintained.

At the thick door of dark hardwood he knocked, once and thrice. Dangling from the doorframe above him, the little silver bell sang: he might enter. He did so slowly, deferentially, not cautiously for the sake of her modesty, for had that been in question, she would not have bidden him enter. He found her standing at a window, eyes cast downward between the thick green curtains—at the courtyard, he realized, where her parents were just departing in their aircarriage. She made no motion, not even to bid them goodbye. They would return by evening, Goodling knew.

In the shadows under the gently domed ceiling he waited impatiently to be acknowledged. He noted that once again she had had the furniture rearranged. Now the sofa stood against the old tapestry on the left wall, and no longer in the center of the room. A third stuffed chair had been added, the trio facing the sofa over a low serving table that now held a coffee set—freshly delivered, for he could smell the rich aroma. It brought a frown to his thin lips: tea was the preferred beverage. The pale floral brocade curtains over the window in the opposite wall had been parted just enough to allow a crack of sunlight into the room. He saw that she was standing just to the side of the lighted area that stretched across the hardwood floor, as if she preferred the shadows. Always a seeker of meaning in portents, he wondered what, if anything, that signified.

At last she turned around. For her apparel on this occasion she had selected a simple gown of pale green gossamer over a long slip of opaque cream, both of which hung from thin shoulder straps. The color of the gown set off her tangerine hair, to which attention was drawn by the headband of woven silver inlaid with bits of polished carnelian. The color of the gemstones was almost lost against the color of her hair.

"You wished," Catalina said, formal, "to see us?"

The majordomo drew a few paces closer. "You are not wearing your lenses," he observed, the rebuke in his tone.

She turned to one side. "They ache our eyes."

"Then I shall have replacements fitted. Milady, have either of your cousins made a pleasing impression on you?"

Her breast trembled with the breath she drew. "Either would provide a marriage of convenience," she replied. "Nothing more."

"A convenient marriage may be necessary—"

She whirled on him, her face hard and her jaw set. "For whom? Certainly not for us! Were it to be Alexor, we should soon exhaust our supply of pumice! Pathor plays croquet poorly, and I despise the game; we should always lose to our parents."

"Your parents will not be around forever, Milady," Goodling pointed out.

"Still he would find a way for us to lose."

He gestured toward a stuffed chair, and a little motion of her hand permitted him to seat himself. "You are not truly vexed by his croquet skills, Milady."

She sighed. "No. No, I am not."

Her lapse from the royal we encouraged him; she might listen to him. But first her mood must be softened.

"There may be alternatives, Milady, found among the lesser relatives," he said carefully. "Someone among them will be able to preserve the bloodline."

Her lips tightened. Still she did not approach him. "It may be as you say, Snarrel, that I shall have to take a lover or two."

"Your mother did."

Catalina gasped. "You never told me that!"

"There was no need to, Milady. In fact, she gave birth."

She sprawled onto a chair, all decorum abandoned. In the silence that followed, she became suspicious. "You are telling me this for a reason," she said. "You always have a reason."

Inwardly Goodling nodded to himself. With Hommer and his team still searching the island for signs of Hoya, he had to plan for the unlikely event that she showed up on Faedra. "The reason is clear, Milady." He spoke now with even greater care. "It is possible that another may lay claim to the throne of Palologa, someone who may feel that her claim is legitimate. I have taken measures, and will take others, to ensure that she is not allowed to present such a claim."

Thoughtful now, Catalina rubbed her chin. "What is the likelihood?"

"For you, Milady, very minor. You need but be aware of this remote possibility, and leave the resolution in my hands."

"In your capable hands. Yes, of course."

She resumed thinking. The expression on her face when she turned to him again sent a tremor through him. "You said 'her claim.' Why not 'his?' What are you not telling me, Majordomo?"

Having a ready answer to that, Goodling relaxed. "I myself do not know the gender of the issue of that relationship. I shall, however, endeavor to learn it. What I can tell you is that this person is no longer on Faedra, nor is there much chance of a return."

"So why then are you worried?" asked Catalina.

He nodded. "Indeed. Why at all?" He stood up, and changed the subject. "I shall see to those lenses immediately, Milady. May I be dismissed?"

"Yes. Yes, of course. And Snarrel...find me someone who hates croquet and has no need of pumicing."

Gravely he inclined his head, and departed.

For a long time Catalina gazed at the door after it had closed. Her mind wandered in a circle that grew smaller and smaller until at last it looped around one singular thought: what was that all about? The seed of a question having been planted, she wondered what else might foster doubts within her.

# 003: Shadows of the Past

Layby orbited an unregistered orange dwarf known among merchants, smugglers, and starwinders as Pitstop. Aside from minor mining projects, several fish smokeries and canneries, and a few breweries and distilleries, Layby featured little of economic consequence. The terrestrial world, 0.86 on the Terran Scale in size and surface gravity, served primarily as a getaway—a place to go for people who wanted to avoid other people, for whatever reason. Personal questions, unless invited or expressly permitted, were considered rude, and sometimes incurred fatal penalties.

Two settlements of note attracted people: Skalder and Viveca, both located on the smallest of Layby's three continents, this one in the temperate zone of the northern hemisphere. The *pied à terre* of Hoya Catalina Palologa, little more than a basic cottage, stood just away from the outskirts of Skalder.

After downdocking at the Skalder Spaceport and paying a modest fee for a private hangar, March let an airfoil take Hoya and Myrrha to the cottage. Following Hoya's directions, they almost passed it by, as it was hidden behind an overgrowth of flowering shrubs, nettings of vines, and a fallen tree. Hoya's arm trembled as she pointed back.

"Turn around," she cried. "That's it! Oh, by the goddesses, what's happened to the place."

"Fourteen years is a lot of time," March said drily, as he swung the airfoil around and onto what had once been a flagstone walkway. The bow pointed where he thought the front entrance should be. He could just make out a door through the dense vegetation. "Does any of that have thorns?" he asked.

Hoya shook her head uncertainly. "I didn't plant anything like that," she said. "No gragens or starnias, anyway." Her face appeared on the verge of tearing up as she climbed down from the airfoil and stood still, regarding the overgrowth. After a few seconds she spread helpless hands. "Oh, what am I going to do?"

"Hire a gardener?" suggested Myrrha.

"Is the door locked?" asked March, peering closer.

"Yes. I mean, I left it that way, I..."

"It's ajar," said Myrrha.

March tested some of the vines and slender branches. "We can get through this," he told them. Drawing the Krupp Stinger from the belt clip, he probed his way into the cottage while the two women waited. After a quick look around, he called out, "I'm not sure you want to see this."

Driven now by his words, Hoya tore a passage through the vegetation, followed closely by Myrrha. The three of them stood together in the front room.

Delicately put, someone had trashed the place. Chair cushions had been gutted, drawers emptied, curtains slashed, tables overturned, legs broken off. The contents of a cooler had been emptied onto the tile floor of the dinette, and so long ago that no odors emanated from the debris. In the rear wall of the front room, two of the three windows had slashed acetate. The doorway off to the right led to the bedroom.

Hoya looked thoroughly forlorn. "I don't know whether I should go in there."

"I'll check it out," said March, and started to move off.

A hand on his elbow stopped him. Rather to his surprise, she spoke with the elegant responsibility of a princess. "No. I have to do it."

"We'll all go, then. Just in case."

The sleeping pad had been gutted, its contents strewn all over the floor. The bed frame, of blond wood, was so much tinder for a fire. Curtains shredded, drawers from the armoire yanked open and turned upside down, the contents dumped on the floor.

Myrrha shook her head in disgust. "What were they looking for?" she wondered.

March toed some debris. "Something small," he guessed.

"But there was nothing here that merited a search," said Hoya.

"That wouldn't matter," March told her, "as long as they thought the item was here."

Even though Hoya had not made an appearance here in fourteen years, she looked distressed. "How long ago, do you think?" she asked.

March slid his fingertips across the front of a drawer, and showed her the dust. "I'd say it's been some time," he said. "Years, perhaps."

"A Palmetto, possibly," said Myrrha. "You might have kept a diary on it."

Hoya made a face, and shook her head.

"In any case, a Palmetto can be hacked," said March. "Not easily, but it can be done." He looked sharply at Hoya. "Did you keep a diary?"

She nodded hesitantly. "But it's safe."

"Where is it?"

"It's...safe."

"I wonder if they found what they were looking for," mused Myrrha.

"I don't think so," March said, looking around again. "There's no obvious stopping point to the search. They even tore out the walls." Again he stared hard at Hoya. "You were last here when you were nine," he said. "Someone would have been with you. Who?"

"Libbelle," Hoya answered. "A lady-in-waiting. But she's dead."

"Dead how?" he asked.

"Well...well..." Hoya looked away. "She was, was killed. It was a robbery; they took her money, her carrybag..."

"They?"

"Well, whoever did it."

"How old was she?"

Angrily Hoya dragged rigid fingers through her hair. "Oh, goddesses, I don't know, why would I know? Mid-thirties, maybe. What does it matter?"

"Maybe they thought she had what they were looking for," said Myrrha. "How long ago was this?"

"Oh, I don't..." Hoya drew a huge breath to steady herself. "Four years ago, on...on Jalune. Can we get out of here? I don't want to see any more."

They began walking toward the door, careful to skirt debris. "We'll find a quiet place to talk," said March. "Something to drink. Coffee, or wine."

"T-talk?"

"Hoya, if I'm..." He glanced apologetically at Myrrha. "If *we're* going to do anything at all for you, I think we need to know the full, complete story. Beginning with where you have been for fourteen years."

She sighed heavily. "Yes. Yes, of course."

\* \* \*

Of the three Families of Wanderby, that of Isaora consisted of the fewest royal personages. Alexor and his parents; two uncles and aunts, and three cousins; and two people who might or might not be related, the issues of relationships that were known but not discussed. One of those was Kamie Isaora.

Despite no official status, Kamie was often referred to but never directly addressed as a cousin of Alexor. For the most part, she kept to her quarters at night and took long hikes during the day when she was not otherwise busy in the House kitchen. She was not consciously avoiding contact with members of the Isaora Family, but she did prefer to keep to herself. There was something about Alexor that bothered her, although she was unable to say what it was. Perhaps it was in the looks he gave her when no one else was watching, or in the snide tone of his soft-spoken words to her. As yet he had not attempted to touch her, but she had little doubt that one day, when the moment was right, he would make an advance.

Now on a hike, she had climbed a hill at the summit of which grew a cluster of yellowbark trees that offered shade from the midday light of Solntsa, Faedra's orange dwarf star. From that vantage point she was able to see distant features of Wanderby. The Fiumal, a river that spilled down from the Trijj Mountains and looped across a flatlands to empty into the Golubic Ocean beyond the limits of her vision. Clots of trees at the bottom of hill slopes, where the runoff from rainfall collected; rows of trees along the riverbanks and along some of the creeks that fed the river. Grass—some soft and lush, some with blades whose edges could slice the skin—grass everywhere, and interspersed with yellow and violet flowers, and tangled vines, and populated by scurrying herbivores and insects who fed there. Birds, ground nests, burrows, nettings of silk erected between plants by whatever fed on whatever was captured in that netting. Kamie loved to watch for movements in the grass, and to wonder what was going to happen next. Often enough, the event was unexpected, and even astonishing.

Like waving to her the other day. Goddesses, how long had it been? She had glimpsed her a few times now and then, but never had the opportunity to speak with her. And what was she doing there? Was she a consort? Had she become a plaything? Not her, please not her...

She had waved back, but only as a return to the greeting. What did that mean?

Seated on the grass at the base of a tree, Kamie drew her knees up and wrapped her arms around them, chin resting on her laced fingers.

Isaora ended at this side of the river, and Palologa began. She might cross over, if she wished; she knew of two shallow fords, easily traversed. She might visit; but not unannounced, for that was unthinkable. She had attended the croquet match without invitation only because Thormin Isaora had wanted his own cook present at the banquet that followed.

And as a result she had spotted her on the balcony only by chance.

Though there had been so little contact over more than a dozen years, Kamie still recognized her. Maybe the red of her hair was a little darker, or it could have been a trick of the shadows on the balcony. She had let it grow; it looked good loose. Kamie wished she had hair like that, long and loose in the wind; hers was a short cap, because she was a kitchen scullery maid, and so black that sunlight gave it blue highlights. And that gown—she had developed to the point where she needed straps. Still, thought Kamie, thinking of her own body, they were almost the same size as mine. If only I had a gown to go with them.

A long sigh eased from Kamie as she took stock of her present outfit. Rough work trousers in faded blue; a simple yellow pullover with thins in the fabric; scuffed brown boots that shod her feet. In her heart she knew that she was not meant for gowns, but for garb similar to what she was now wearing. This was how she saw herself —externally. As for who she really was inside, that was a work in progress. One thing was certain: her old friend on the balcony needed help. She meant to find a way to be there for her.

# 004: Ruminations

Snarrel, thought Hommer, as his foot scuffed at the crushed grass, was not going to like this, not at all.

Four depressions in the grass, each one at the corner of a rectangle, the spacing indicative of the support pods of a small spacecraft, probably a 'skip. Another depression, this one larger and longer, in the center of the rectangle, where the underside of the ship had rested. Because the grass had only just begun to recover, Hommer estimated that no more than three days had lapsed since the downdock.

The campfire site his searchers had located, some fifty meters away, had been dead that long as well. It had been extinguished by dousing it with water. There was nothing to indicate how many individuals had sat around it.

They had also found a Palmetto, or what remained of one. It had been adapted to emit a distress signal, and almost certainly had belonged to Hoya Catalina Palologa. But it was no longer functional, the battery having fried, and whatever had been stored on it was illegible. Still, Hommer had it placed in a container to take back to Goodling. Perhaps something could be read from it. But he now had no doubt that Hoya Catalina was alive and well...and somewhere else.

He was not looking forward to delivering his report.

To Hommer's complete astonishment, Snarrel Goodling took the news of Hoya Catalina's survival and disappearance calmly enough. The majordomo was seated, not on his raised chair, but comfortably on the sofa, sipping from a mug of tea now and then as he listened to Hommer's report. When the minion had finished, he said nothing for long enough that Hommer, nervous, threw a couple glances over his shoulder, looking for whoever was coming to get him.

Finally Goodling indicated the serving set on the low table in front of the sofa. "Would you care for some tea?" he asked.

Hommer stammered at the unprecedented offer. "I-I...well, yes, Majordomo, if...if..."

A casual wave of Goodling's hand invited Hommer to help himself. "And please, sit down," he said. "That chair, if you wish."

Still apprehensive, Hommer seated himself. He had to admit the tea was excellent, and with Goodling drinking it from the same pot, it could not be poisoned.

"A small craft," Goodling mused, "suggests one that is privately owned. It's likely the owner was drawn by the distress signal, but of course we cannot even guess the motivation for the response. Conformity to space law? A scavenger? Someone willing to help? In any case, she was taken somewhere. She would have complained about her situation on Calla Cried, probably officially. Yet we have heard nothing so far." He peered at Hommer. "What does that suggest to you?"

The minion blinked. "Majordomo?"

"Come, Satrin, think! She has thus far issued no official complaint."

Hommer's tongue flicked across his lips. "She...she means to respond personally?"

"That certainly is a possibility," Goodling agreed. "But to do that, she has to return here."

"So...so we monitor Faedra's two spaceports?"

"Obviously. But she does not have to downdock at one." He warmed his tea from the pot, and sat back. "We still have not located her *Zelena*, her 'skip. We will continue to search, of course, but we must begin to watch for it here."

"I shall assign Eyes, Majordomo."

"But she may arrive on another vessel," Goodling pressed. "Conceivably one operated by her rescuer."

"Yes, of course."

"Finish your tea, Satrin. Then begin." He considered briefly, and added, as if in an afterthought, "On your way out, stop by the kitchen and tell Hallia that I wish to see her now, and that she is excused from her duties for the rest of the day."

\* \* \*

On this occasion Goodling managed to accomplish what he wanted with the scullery maid without any marks showing on her fair skin. In her dark gray-brown eyes he basked in the hatred and loathing there. Nothing would please her more than to kill him, slowly. But that would require an action that was not within her to perform. He savored that failing in her, as he savored the remnants of the fragrant incense still emanating from the small brazier at the side of the sofa. Weakness only made her more appealing.

After a final look he dismissed Hallia as he might have dismissed a helpless insult—words of no account. Her back was rigid as she trod toward the door, the remains of her clothing over her arm, the hem of the burlap gown he had provided her now swirling about her knees with each stride she took. She did not glance back before she shut the door—gently, for in that manner it carried a rebuke far more powerful than slamming it might have done.

Only then, after he had assuaged his anger and frustration by the use of her body did his thoughts return to the problem at hand. Impossible to know how it had all gone so wrong, so swiftly. Hoya Catalina gone? When she should have been dead, and dead long before this? In retrospect, he should have killed her outright. He had feared that the marks left by killing her would betray the act, should she be found, and place all who knew her under suspicion, something that might well disrupt his plans. Had she starved to death, marooned on a remote and unfrequented world, it would have far better served his purposes. With matters as they stood now, he was left with little choice other than to find Hoya and kill her—or have someone kill her...

Again he considered possibilities. Assassins were always available for a price. Secrecy was part of their code of honor—none would ever reveal the identity of a contractor, for to do so would spark distrust throughout the profession. In most instances, the assassin was completely unaware of that identity, as the contract was brokered by the guild. What mattered was the payment to one's bank account, usually held at the Bank of Relay. Goodling knew of several adept Guild assassins, including Marzanna, whom he had employed on a couple of occasions. A strange *nom de travail*, he thought, wondering about the name's origins. But it could be of no great concern: an assassin by any other name was an assassin. Resolved now, he nodded to himself. It was time to release some of his private funds to the Assassins Guild.

\* \* \*

Hoya Palologa had one more place to stop before she spoke to March regarding her past. Alone in the guest stateroom, she divested herself of garments and stepped into the shower stall in the hygiene alcove, under a fine spray of water set as hot as she could stand it. Streams pelted her upper back, and rivulets plummeted down her spine and legs. Eyes closed, she inclined her head forward so that water warmed her cheeks and spilled from her chin. For long moments she held this position, letting the spray take with it the remains of the day. Draining her of weariness, it allowed her to relax, and to gather herself.

In that steamy moment of perfect clarity, she decided not to present March with the full truth. A rogue he might be, and untrustworthy, but even someone like him would have to act on the knowledge he gained. She would have to find herself a plausible past for him.

Almost absently she reached for the scrubbing pad and the bar of rose-scented soap, and began to lather and cleanse herself. Some events she might be able to disclose to him, such as the mistake and subsequent abduction that had led to her being deposited, sedated, on Calla Cried. Even as that occurred to her, thoughts of that dark day were shunted aside, leaving only a vague residue. She had meant to quietly visit a childhood friend of hers in Isaora House, entering through a hidden entrance in the rear of the castle, but before the encounter she had been betrayed. A hard rap on the back of the head by an unseen hand had deprived her of consciousness. She had awakened on Calla Cried, beside a supply of food that might, if carefully husbanded, last her for half a year. But how had her assailant known of her visit? Had the friend betrayed her? Who...who? Attacked soundlessly from behind, she had seen no one. A ragged sound of frustration shot from her mouth as she turned her face to the spray.

Hoya had been glad enough to be sent away to school and to university. Even at the age of nine, when she had departed Palologa House, she had become at least aware that there were machinations going on within the family that she knew little about. Although she rarely glanced back over her shoulder, she always had the feeling that she ought to do so. Schooling, however, mitigated the absence from her parents, although she did sometimes miss the labyrinthine passageways inside the castle, where she could hide herself away for a while. Now, fourteen years later, and under the spray of soothing hot water, she wondered why she had ever felt the need to hide. A sixth sense, perhaps, had spoken to her then of intrigue; she did not now know. But it mattered, because she was still being pursued by her past.

Let them come, she grated silently to herself, as she shut off the water. They don't know me now.

# 005: End of the Road

The star around which Grenadine revolved was white on the verge of green, a type F1 that had bossed its system of five planets for a mere two billion years, scarcely enough time for a complex ecology to have evolved on any of them. The fourth in the system, Grenadine knew oceans, fish and algae analogs, and terrestrial flowering plants, among other fauna and flora, but nothing that might be regarded as even borderline intelligent. The arrival of humanity altered that state only a little. The principal human activity was mining—scheelite, vanadinite, chromite, and some of the rare earths. Those who labored in the mines often had spotty backgrounds—fugitives for the most part, for one reason or another, wanted for infractions of the law or of propriety, and others outright convicts unable or unwilling to find work in easier settings.

Even before the *Bluebolt* downdocked at Vanfeller Spaceport, March wondered why Hoya Palologa had chosen a *pied à terre* on a world where at any moment violence might erupt for the slimmest of reasons. Servile women and girls were welcome; while several characteristics applied to Hoya, servility was in no way among them. Advances were made on her and Myrrha as they accompanied March through the small terminal on the way to let an airfoil. All were rebuffed, although clearly a few of the men were unwilling to take rejection well. Hands on sidearms clipped to belts served to clarify the meaning of, "No"—March found even himself chagrined by a couple of approaches—and the trio soon emerged unscathed into the bright midday sunshine, with no one in amorous pursuit.

"There," said Hoya, pointing to a squat structure of basalite blocks roofed with terracotta tiles. Several airfoils rested on tarmac in front of the office, making the sign of

"Airfoils For Hire" somewhat redundant. Beside the building stood a refreshment kiosk with an overhang that shaded a pair of round white tables and attendant chairs, all at the moment unoccupied. The ambient temperature encouraged the trio to take a break there before broaching their transportation requirements. Hoya, familiar with the kiosk, placed orders, while March and Myrrha took up chairs.

"She's very secretive here," said Myrrha, keeping her voice down. "She knows where she is going, but won't tell us."

"There's an aphorism about books and covers," he replied.

"It's not a bad-looking cover."

March barked a dry laugh. "You find her attractive?"

"Were she of such a mind, she would be a new experience for me. But...no, I think not. I don't know enough about her." Pointedly she added, "And neither do you."

"I stand rebuked without cause."

"As may be." Myrrha looked up. "At least she bought us drinks."

The beverages proved to be shaved ice with flavoring. They toasted one another perfunctorily and without words, and March, with prior experience, sipped carefully and allowed most of the ice to melt in his mouth before swallowing. He noticed that Hoya drank along the same lines, while Myrrha guzzled a good quarter of her own. He started to caution her against aches in her chest and head, and stopped himself. It was easy to forget that despite her appearance she was not human, but a computer simulation.

"You're wrong," Myrrha told him, reading his expression. "I told you: I *am* human. But as a computer I can manage my physiological responses."

"I'll try to control my expressions," he replied, though he doubted he would ever be able to do so well enough to make himself illegible to her.

She shook her head. "The human thing to do would have been to warn me about the ice, March. Even though it does not affect me that way." She sighed. "I wish you would understand that."

Hoya looked from one to the other and back. "What are you two on about?" To Myrrha, she added, her eyes hard with disbelief, "And you're a what? A computer?"

"It's complicated," Myrrha told her, and dismissed the question with a shake of her head. "Thank you for the drinks. I was afraid it would be coffee. In this heat..." She left that thought unfinished.

Hoya shivered. "I loathe coffee. How can you be a —"

"How far is it to your cottage from here?" March asked, before Hoya could pursue the matter further.

"Around twenty kilometers," Hoya replied, still examining Myrrha as if for signs and portents. "Half an hour. If it is still there, of course." At length she turned to him, and appeared to be on the verge of a statement. Her lips even parted for a second or two. But the moment passed, and she resumed addressing her drink.

March scowled at her, but withheld comment. A glance at Myrrha told him that she had noticed the change of heart as well. Once more he found himself lamenting the decision to assist Hoya. Too much about her was clandestine, probably concealed among tangles of half-truths, and he now expected it to remain so. Perhaps she would have a change of heart when they reached the cottage, but he placed no reliance on that. Still, they were here on Grenadine. There was nothing left to do but finish the refreshment and let an airfoil, and go find out something else about Hoya that he would have to unlearn.

\* \* \*

Perhaps having indulged in spicy foods, Justinio Palologa sprawled in a sitting-room chair with his right hand over the aching area of his stomach. Dyspepsia had struck him more often of late; he had been attended to by a physician who assured him that his digestive tract was operating within normal parameters. It was small comfort that their official taster never showed any ill-effects; nor did Olena. He resolved to consume fewer peppery dishes, knowing that he would probably forget the resolution, as usual.

After a satisfying belch, he patted his stomach, and got up to stand by the window that gave onto the flatlands of Wanderby. At the moment, there was nothing to see, but Justinio was not looking for anything. His eyes glazed over, unfocused, and his mind wandered to Catalina, one day to be Duchess. As a child of ten she had decided to change the name by which she was familiarly addressed, from Hoya to Catalina. She had always been willful, but over her adolescent years she had mellowed. The time was past due for her to have a consort. Goodling would simply have to look harder, and perhaps expand his scope to include lesser relatives.

Another matter weighed on the Duke, now that his thoughts regarding Catalina had settled themselves. Over two decades ago, a year before the birth of Hoya Catalina, his wife had given birth to a daughter he had not sired. Now, as on previous occasions, he wondered what had happened to her. Being of the bloodline, she could not be abandoned to the villages. Instead, he had relied on the majordomo to arrange a good household for her. To protect her, he had arranged to keep her true identity a secret, and so the girl was raised as an Isaora household servant. But now that Justinio considered the matter, he realized that he had not seen her in quite some time. He would have to inquire after her with Goodling.

Curiously, Justinio felt ill at ease about such an inquiry—as if he did not truly wish to know the answers to his questions. At length he turned away from the window; his stomach, like his spirit, had calmed. He wondered who among his household was up for a bit of croquet.

* * *

The distance to Hoya's *pied à terre* proved to be close to seventy kilometers from Vanfeller Spaceport. March found himself unsurprised by Hoya's deception—seventy being far more than the twenty she had assured him. She seemed to be going out of her way to keep him off-balance, almost as if this were a calculated plan. But he was unable to guess what she might gain by it.

Not only was the distance underestimated, but the terrain they had to cross was rugged for an airfoil. Some titan had deliberately scattered boulders over the dry land, and March, deftly piloting the conveyance, had to skirt or override many of them. Gullies and ravines were laden with dust and fine white sand that the fanblades roused and swept up against the plexishield, obscuring his vision. Why Hoya would have wanted to stay in such a desolate land was beyond him. By the time they arrived, the effort and the tension of cautious operation left him fatigued and drenched in sweat. He wanted a drink and a nap, and knew he was not about to get either.

The Grenadine cottage was in worse shape than the one on Layby. Little remained of the structure, some of which had collapsed in on itself. March saw less furniture overall, and supposed whatever had survived more or less intact had already been taken by scavengers. Hoya herself appeared less disquieted, as if she had anticipated the condition of the cottage.

"How long has it been since you were here?" asked Myrrha.

Hoya gave her an absent look, and spoke as if from a distance. "About six years. It was a new place; I had it built the year before."

March kicked at a bit of debris as he scanned about. The cottage was not alone in the area—three others were in the range of his vision, none within half a kilometer, and all appearing to be intact. He lifted a few broken sheets of wind-worn wallboard and found more debris under them. If the searchers had located what they were looking for, the signs of that discovery were beyond his ability to perceive. Coming here had been something of a fool's errand.

He started to say as much, but Myrrha, reading him, stopped him with a hand on his arm.

"I'm sorry, Hoya," she said. "Was there anything here of value?"

The slow way in which Hoya shook her head said that she had scarcely heard the question. She muttered something under her breath.

Immediately Myrrha said, "Enough, Hoya. Tell us something!"

Hoya glanced up. Already the sun was hot, and had yet to reach the midday mark. She spoke haltingly. "There are...reasons for...certain people to look for me."

"Who?" yelled March. With great effort he resisted the urge to shake her. "Who, dammit?"

"We should seek shelter," she said coolly. "We are done here. Please remote your spaceskip to this location. I will arrange for someone to retrieve the airfoil. Please set a course for Narva, for the Narvene Spaceport, and drop me off there. I will pay you for your help, and I will not trouble you further."

# 006: Seductions

"I am going to wed Catalina Palologa," Alexor Isaora declared to Kamie. "So if you are nice to me, I can improve your lot."

Kamie had been chopping onions. Even as Alexor had entered the kitchen, she had begun hammering the blade at the unfortunate vegetable on the cutting board, irritation powering the muscles in her arm. She knew why he had entered; for the next hour, while Jinzy was on break and the afternoon crew was not due to arrive until later, she was alone in the kitchen. No witnesses, she thought. Just the way he likes it.

Alexor took a tentative step toward her; she backed away, the knife lowered to her side. He reached toward the top button of her blouse. Kamie held her breath. If he touched her, she would...she would...

"Let's see them," he said, his tone hard. "I want to look at them."

Lips taut, she shook her head violently.

"I am the invested Prince of Corrik, and heir to the Isaora Throne," he grated severely. "And I will look at your mams."

The crudity shocked Kamie. She started to back away, but his hand snagged her blouse and ripped the top button free. Aghast, she finally managed a step, only to abut a counter. She had nowhere to go.

Sensing victory, Alexor reached again for her blouse. Up swept her knife hand, and back down to bring the knife against his extended arm. The razor-sharp blade, awash with onion juice, sliced open his bare forearm.

The heir to the Isaora Throne swore viciously as he jerked his arm back, free hand clamped over the stinging wound. Already blood was streaming between his fingers as he cradled the limb against his belly. Cries of anguish fled him as he staggered toward the kitchen entrance.

Kamie did not draw a breath until the door had swung shut behind him. In temporary relief she slumped against the counter, gasping for air. It took a long moment for the enormity of what she had done to register. Her dove-gray eyes, dulled by apprehension, looked this way and that, as if to seek refuge. But she would have nowhere to go, once word of the incident became known. Nowhere to go, unless she departed immediately, without even taking time to pack.

* * *

Narva, like many other worlds inhabited by humans, was nominally administered with a blind eye to other events. Thus it was that the average Narvite was safe and secure at home, at work, or shopping, but if questionable indulgences were desired, they were available, for a price, and if one knew where to look. Newcombe March, who had visited Narva on several occasions that involved shipments of dubious origin, knew where to look. Accordingly, upon downdocking, he escorted Myrrha and Hoya—somewhat against the latter's will—to a quiet subterranean cubbyhole known as *The Locker*, where private booths were available for good food and for conversation meant only for the ears of those in the booth. Such privacy was guaranteed by a pair of armed guards who brooked no violations.

The tavern itself consisted of an open bay with four benched tables arranged at the corners of a rectangle, and rows of separate curtained booths along three of the walls. The fourth wall supported the serving and drinking counter, and was operated by two serving maids and an assistant manager. On the other side of that wall was the kitchen, a storage room, and the manager's office. Covering the entire establishment was a ceiling of open, rough-hewn rafters. Above that, at ground level, spread a public park.

Recognized immediately, March was welcomed by a comely serving maid named Sheruthe as he descended the last of the creaky wooden steps. A hard hug followed the welcome, an amiable glance at his two companions included them simply because they were in his company. It was unthinkable that Sheruthe would inquire after them. Casually March looked around; only a few patrons sat at the tables and on stools at the counter—seven in all, and none that he recognized. The evening was late, and although *The Locker* remained open at all hours, he doubted attendance would increase substantially during his visit.

Short black wrap swishing gently with each step she took, Sheruthe led them to a corner booth at the rear of the open bay. March watched her walk until Myrrha elbowed his ribs, at which point he shifted the focus of his senses from his eyes to his nose, taking in the aromas of alcohol, tobacco, hot oil, grilled meat, and blends of spice and herb, garlic and fresh rosemary prominent among them.

At the booth, Sheruthe used her Palmetto to activate the heavy, dark red curtain; it slid aside to show that no one was within—a mandatory propriety of *The Locker*. After the three seated themselves—the two women facing March across the table—she invited their orders. March and Myrrha ordered Augsburger Dark to start with, and the sauerbraten in half an hour.

Hoya Catalina, still unhappy, said, "I think tea, please. A Viridian blend, if you have it. Something herbal."

Sheruthe nodded; her hands swept short black tresses from her forehead. To March, she said, "It's good to see you again," and closed the curtain.

"Tea," said March, not quite sardonically.

"I prefer it." Hoya glanced at the curtain. "It seems she knows you."

"She gives me good service."

"So I would wager."

Myrrha drummed fingertips on the tabletop. "That remark ill becomes you, Milady."

Hoya looked contrite. "Yes. Yes, of course it does." She hung her head, just a little. "I apologize, March. Just...tell me why I am here. As soon as I pay you, we're done."

"So you said. But I wish to talk. And it is safe to do so here. There is a sound dampening field enclosing this booth. I could scream, and no one would hear me."

She looked doubtful. "Those who are looking for me would be able to bypass that field."

"Perhaps," Myrrha agreed. "But first they would have to know you were here in *The Locker*. How would they know that? Your Palmetto, or what remains of it, is on Calla Cried; your shuttle is elsewhere on Narva. No, Milady, whatever you tell us will not leave this booth."

"What makes you think the *Zelena* is on Narva?"

Myrrha shrugged. "Else why are we here?"

A light chuckle escaped Hoya. "I thought you were supposed to be a computer."

"Oh very well." Myrrha sat back, and turned to face her. "I calculate a ninety-two point seven seven three zero four percent probability that your shuttle is here." She counted off the reasons on the tips of her fingers. "One, you wanted to be brought here, and left here. This strongly suggests ready access to transportation elsewhere. Two, you are better served by independence of movement, especially as you withhold disclosure of the identity of your pursuers. This too suggests your own transportation. Three, you claim you will pay us for our help, yet you have no money save the change you received from the thalers we gave you to purchase drinks on Grenadine. As you also have neither fundscard nor Palmetto access to an account, this suggests a cache of cash—pardon me for that—somewhere here on Narva. What safer place to conceal it than aboard a secured ship?

Four, given that you are being pursued, and you have no weapons, it is logical to suppose that you have one or more aboard the *Zelena*. Five, I might even calculate that the shuttle is nearby, and close to the spaceport, as you have at present no means of soliciting transportation and must therefore walk to its location."

Myrrha raised her hand with all five fingers spread, and considered for a moment. "Six," she went on, growing another finger.

Hoya emitted a short scream and drew away from her. "By the goddesses!" she croaked. "You...you *are*...but you're impossible!"

Myrrha smiled. "March tells me that all the time."

Hoya sputtered. "But...but..."

"Take a few breaths and relax," March told her.

Myrrha went on, unperturbed. "I gave you an erroneous percent, Milady. The decimal should have been point seven seven three zero five. I neglected to carry the one." Eyes the color of polished jade glistened with humor, though she kept a straight face. "I've always had a bit of a problem with ones."

"You," Hoya finally managed. "You're a computer."

Myrrha shook her head. "Not so. I am a computer-generated and fully-human individual who has retained all her computer capabilities." She leaned a little closer to Hoya, and spoke with gentle urgency. "What I am, is March's companion, in whatever form necessary or desirable. Albeit reluctantly at first, he has taken on your situation. He is very dogged; so am I. If you want our help, we will help you. But we need to know what to do, and that means knowing what the problem is. You've been told this before. Now is the time to make your best decision."

But," said Hoya, a prelude to a protest, and stopped. For a moment she seemed lost. "But then why are you, why are you green?"

"I like green."

"But...if I understand you correctly, you chose to be this color. It is not what I first thought, the result of body tint or hair dye or eye lenses. You truly are green."

"If you wish me to alter it, I will. Blue, yellow, sepia, purple..." She thought for a moment. "I've never tried purple. Perhaps..."

"I give up," sighed Hoya.

A silver bell tinkled high overhead. March touched a pad on the wall, and the curtain retracted. Sheruthe had brought their beverages.

\*    \*    \*

At first Kamie Isaora had no destination in mind when she set out in the general direction of the hill where she had dallied the day before. Torn between trudging in despair and striding to put distance between herself and the Isaora castle, she meandered this way and that, now following the course of a small brook, now entering a defile that took her between clumps of topolla trees, here stepping over a scattering of stones, there balancing herself along the crest of an outcrop. Splotches of fine dust attached themselves to cheeks damp with perspiration. Tears carved pathways through those splotches, only to end up at the point of her jaw and then onto the sparse grass. Crying, because now she was lost to the life she had led, and did not know what the next step or the next moment would bring.

Presently Kamie took shade under the spreading boughs of a harper tree, so-called because of the whistle of a breeze made as it passed through thin leaves with sharp edges. There was a breeze at the moment, and above her hovered a plaintive melody that matched the mood of her heart. Eyes shut, she leaned back against the smooth trunk, and let the tune soothe her. Twice she caught herself nodding off. The exhaustion she felt was not physical; her daily walks kept her in shape. But her emotions had been wrung out like a dishrag, leaving her with a lump of nothing at all.

The breeze dried her skin. With the edge of her hand she scraped the dust splotches from her cheeks. Her dove-gray eyes took in her attire: blouse with a button missing, dark brown trousers, boots dull with old grease. A laundry bag held several items she had taken from the kitchen: two tins of smoked fish, some grain bars, a set of eating utensils, and a sieve. She had no idea why she had taken the sieve. She had not been thinking clearly at the time. In her pockets she carried a Palmetto, an identification card, and a pouch of coins—two gold, seven silver, and six bronze. She had nothing else.

"Except my freedom," she soughed. At the moment it did not feel like much of an asset.

Abruptly Kamie sat up straight. *You're better than this*, she told herself. *Consider what you need most: a place to live, and a place to work.*

She shook her head. *No, what I need most is a friend.*

*But I'm not going to get any of that by sitting around here.*

She willed herself to stand up. The nearest village, Carrikdove, lay west by the coast of a bay, a good two hours' hike away. She placed one foot in front of the other. After that, it got easier.

# 007: Lost and Found

Hoya Catalina began with the most recent circumstance.  She had a friend in Isaora Castle with whom she had kept in sporadic contact during her long absence from Faedra.  On impulse, and at an open moment in her life, she had informed this friend of her intent to visit.  She knew a secret passage into the castle, having used it previously as a child, and asked to be met there.  After locating the entrance to the subterranean labyrinth, she crept silently through once-familiar passageways until she reached the central corridor and the alcove where she was to be met. But she did not make it to the alcove.

"I should have looked," said Hoya. "I should have been more cautious.  The only security precaution I took was to arrive on Faedra in a commercial transport, rather than my own 'skip, in which I was known.  I simply did not anticipate trouble.  At the very worst, if caught, I should have been delivered to Palologa Castle and my parents.  The lighting was minimal, although that is no excuse.  Out of the corner of my eye I saw a shadow of movement, and I knew it was already too late.  A blow to my head rendered me unconscious.  When I came to, I was on Calla Cried. You know the rest of that story."

"Who is this friend?" March asked.

Hoya stared at her empty teacup, and refilled it from the carafe. "It's the obvious question, I know. But she wouldn't..." Her chest rose and fell with a sad sigh. "Her name is Kamie Isaora.  She works in the kitchen; she's a kitchen maid.  But she's...there's something about her, and I don't know what it is, or even how to describe it."

"She betrayed you," said Myrrha.

"I concede that it appears that way.  But no, Kamie wouldn't, not ever. That cannot be the answer."

"But you said she was the only one who knew," March reminded her. "Given your facts, there is no other explanation."

"I know, I know. Don't you think that has been tearing at me? But it's not her."

"So who hit you?" asked Myrrha.

"I don't know."

"And why would they dump you on Calla Cried?"

"I don't know." She pursed her lips, thinking. "To die, of course. I only lived that long because I saw to my food intake, and managed to augment that with hunting and gathering. But why would they want me dead? And if they wanted me dead, why not just kill me outright? They certainly had the opportunity."

"If we find out why," said March, "I imagine we'll know who." He drained the last of his ale. "All right, let's move on. You said you were sent away to school when you were nine, and that you had not returned to Faedra before visiting Kamie Isaora. Why not?"

"I am the heir to the throne," Hoya answered, readily enough. "A well-rounded education is *de rigueur* for the position."

"Which university?" he asked.

"Margent."

He blew a sigh through puffed lips. "That's way out in the Fringes."

"I know. It was thought best to put a lot of distance between me and the throne."

Myrrha pounced. "Who thought it best? Your parents?"

"No. Snarrel Goodling. He's our—"

"Majordomo, yes," said March. "Did he say why?"

Hoya shrugged. "I am the heir. There are people who would be interested in that fact. Out in the Fringes, no one would know me. I might study without incident."

"That makes sense," he allowed. "But you graduated two years ago. Why not come home?"

"I...was working."

"Doing what?" asked Myrrha.

"This and that. Menial jobs. I wanted to know what it was like to be, well, one of my subjects. I wanted that experience. And I could not get that in Wanderby."

Myrrha's upper incisors worried at her lower lip. "I think...I need another ale," she said, and pulled the cord for service.

"Some of those menial tasks must have been rough," observed March, after the second round of drinks had been delivered. Following a perfunctory toast, like Myrrha, he drank directly from the bottle. "I mean, your nose. And there's a scar on your upper left arm."

"Oh. No," Hoya said easily. "My nose was broken the first year in school on Margent, when I was ten. I was the new student, and a boy thought I should share my desert. It was chocolate cake, worth fighting for. I lost." She looked wistful, thinking back, and spoke quietly. "That time, I lost. It was...a lesson. Even though I had revealed nothing of my background, I still assumed that as the Duke's daughter I was entitled to respect and protection. Over that first year and into the second, I learned that Life doesn't care who you are. You have to take care of yourself. Once I established that, I ate my chocolate cake."

The simple maturity of the statement impressed March, and he became aware that Myrrha was watching him closely. Although they had nothing to do with chocolate, he had learned some of the same lessons. Life was an entity with whom one had to reach an understanding; once that was settled, it did not get any easier, but it did become clearer. He found himself regarding Hoya with fresh eyes.

But uncertainty remained, for she had not volunteered the cause of the scar on her arm. He knew she had suffered a crease from the beam of an energy weapon, he knew that because he himself had two of them, one across the right ribs, the other on the left hip. But he decided not to press the issue. White deceptions were one matter; he was more interested in her dark side.

"And you've had no contact with your parents since you were sent away fourteen years ago?" asked Myrrha, pursuing the obvious.

Hoya's shoulders rose and fell, a shrug that spoke of a lack of concern. "Infrequent messages left on my Palmetto during the first two...three years. Twice I spoke with my mother during that time. Nothing since then. I did leave a few messages, but never received any responses. After a while, I lost myself in my education, and in a few friendships. I accepted that it was my parents' job, their duty, to produce an heir; it was the task of others to rear and nurture it. So it was enough that I was the heir. Eventually my moment would arrive...or I would be recalled."

"But you wanted to see Kamie Isaora," March reminded her.

"I missed her," Hoya said simply. But her expression twisted. "Which was odd," she said absently.

"In what way, odd?" pressed Myrrha.

But Hoya shook her head against the question, as if previously she had asked it of herself, without arriving at an answer.

The arrival of the sauerbraten and spaetzle temporarily ended the inquiry.

\* \* \*

By the time Kamie Isaora reached Carrikdove, Solntsa was poised just above the horizon, already a fading orange amid a streak of pink and salmon clouds. But it cast her shadow behind her; she thought that was auspicious. It lifted her spirits as she took in the scene before her. There was only one glideway through the settlement, and it led directly to the sea. Simple houses of wood and cut stone stood on the south half of Carrikdove;

small business enterprises occupied the other. Kamie had been here several times on errands for the kitchen—the primary commercial activity was fishing, and the Isaora Family was fond of grilled syomga. Twice Jinzy had accompanied her...

Dismayed, Kamie came to a stop just outside the village limits. She had not spoken with Jinzy about her departure. Worse, far worse, she had left the girl to the clutchings of Alexor Isaora. Helplessness settled onto her like a weighted net from which she was unable to struggle free. That there was nothing she could do for Jinzy made her shoulders ache with a pain she could not simply shrug away.

Move, she told herself, girt with determination, and she attended the end of her flight. As she approached, a few children played incomprehensible games with a red and white ball, and a couple of brown and black dogs chased one another across unfenced yards. Here and there on porches sat adults, watching, talking, smoking cheroots. Only one or two paid Kamie the slightest attention as she trod the edge of the glideway. In the waters ahead a pair of fishing boats gently bobbed in the waves.

The lights of a tavern invited Kamie. If nothing else, she needed a place to rest and think. Taverns were not noted for their quiet atmosphere, but she thought that perhaps a room upstairs for the night would suit her, and clearly this structure of yellow stone and dark wood had two levels. A sign dangling from a post identified the establishment as *The Parsley Sprig*. She made for the tavern, and hesitated at the door, ears keened for sounds of revelry—she was, after all, a young woman alone. All she detected was a sporadic murmur, as if a server were discussing an order. She tugged the door open and stepped in out of the twilight.

Without several small tables scattered about the open bay, the interior reminded Kamie a little of one of the drawing rooms in the Isaora castle. A few people sat about, in conversation or in solitary drinking. They looked up when she entered, gave her a quick view, and returned to their chosen activities. Breathing a little sigh of relief, she stepped up to the serving counter and perched on a stool to await notice by the barkeeper. She was a sturdy woman on the verge of middle age, perhaps in her early eighties, and dressed for work in trousers and a flannel shirt fronted by a stained white apron. Her short brown hair was showing a bit of gray, and her deepset eyes seemed to be aware of everything. At the moment, she was porting four froth-topped mugs to a pair of tables near the window in the front corner of the bay. Still she had time to acknowledge Kamie's presence with a curt nod.

Kamie sat patiently, and finally the woman approached. The name tag on her apron read GARLA. She said, slightly rushed, "What'll it be, *meela*?"

The gentle endearment, friendly-meant from a much older woman, caught Kamie off-guard. Indecisive at first, she asked for an ale, which was drawn and delivered.

"That'll be a bronze, *meela*," said Garla. But as she looked at Kamie, something gave her pause. She tilted her head to one side, preparatory to a question. "Are you all right? You look...down."

"It's a long story," said Kamie.

"And I'm rushed. But I'm almost caught up. And like all tavern keeps, I listen good and keep secrets. Just give me a minute or two."

Kamie relaxed further. Unaccustomed as she was in general to people who minded their own business or were genuinely friendly, she now felt that she might have come to the right place. There remained only to obtain lodging for the night. Already she was planning in the morning to go down to the docks and look for work.

Within five minutes and half her mug of ale, she was facing Garla across the counter again. She started to pull a bronze coin from her pouch, but the barkeep's hand stayed her. "No, *meela*, you look like you've walked a light-year or two, and there's not a lot of jingle in that pouch. Now, are you all right?"

"I am," answered Kamie. "I will be. I was wondering...can I let a room upstairs for—"

But Garla rushed off to answer a summons for drinks.

The tavern, already quiet, moved toward silence as three men departed. Presently Garla returned to the counter. "You were inquiring after a room for the night, I believe," she said. "Those I can't comp you, and it's a gold a night."

"I have it," said Kamie, and laid one on the counter. "I know you're busy, so I can see myself up, but I'll need a key."

"Already in the door lock," she said. "Pick the room you want; they're all unoccupied except mine. You might try Seven, though. That was my pastdaughter's room. She left some clothes behind..."

"Thank...thank you."

Garla scanned the bay, but the four remaining patrons, obviously fishermen, indicated no immediate needs.

"It's been a rush like this for five days now," Garla went on, her voice burred by weariness. "Ever since school ended for the trake season. I had a student working here, and my pastdaughter filled in on occasion, but after graduation they took off for a future in the stars. I suppose they'll settle someplace when they're ready." She glanced at the Palmetto below the counter. "Time for me to start washing some of the mugs."

"Wait," said Kamie, her mouth ahead of her brain. "I-I can do that."

For a long moment, Garla inspected her. Finally she gave a little nod. "It's not much silver and bronze, *meela*, but the room and meals are comp, unless you eat like an akoola. And this is a relatively slow night."

"I worked in a kitchen before I came here."

"Better. But you're not working this evening. You're exhausted. Go on upstairs and take your room. We start setting up an hour after sunrise."

Wiping tears from her eyes, Kamie finished her ale and went upstairs, her footsteps lighter now.

# 008: Independence

With the repast finished, little discussion followed in the booth in *The Locker*. After ordering one more round of drinks, March went back to the point where the inquiry had broken off. To get Hoya talking again, he chose a non-threatening topic.

"What was your primary field of study?" he asked her.

"General studies," she replied. "A little of that. As a Duchess, I would have no need of a specialty, except perhaps in formal etiquette." She leaned closer, and whispered conspiratorially. "Truth be known, I could not care less where the salad forks go."

"To the immediate left of the dinner forks," Myrrha said smugly.

Hoya smothered a laugh. "Yes, thank you." She rose from the bench. "I'm going to the alcove."

"I'll alert the GalaxyNet," Myrrha said drily.

"I'll be back," she said, and slipped around the edge of the curtain.

"She drank an entire pot of tea," said March. "She may be a moment or two."

"Probably," agreed Myrrha.

"What's your assessment so far?"

"Everything is plausible and insufficient." She turned her mug around and around. "I understand her parents' rationale in letting others raise their daughter. It's not an unusual practice in royalty. But it doesn't ring quite true, and I cannot tell you why. Plausible, as I said. And menial tasks? She hires things done; she does not do them herself, and risk her fingernails."

March pursed his lips and nodded. "Maybe."

"Yes. And maybe I'm being unfair. But I'll say this: if she is not the heir to the throne, she's very, very good."

"Too good?"

"That's the question, isn't it?"

A few quiet minutes of waiting passed. Myrrha remained calm, while March fought back increasing agitation. At last he said, "We'd better go check the hygiene alcove."

Myrrha's hand arrested him. "I'll go," she said, rising from the bench. "A man should not interrupt a lady at her toilet."

"You made that up."

"I certainly did not," she shot back, mock indignation in her tone. "It's right after the page about salad forks."

The silver bell chimed. Both March and Myrrha stared up at it. Cautiously, not knowing whom to expect to see, but hoping for the best while expecting the worst, he opened the curtain.

Sheruthe, somewhat perturbed, handed him an envelope bearing the logo of *The Locker*. "She left this for you."

March thanked her and closed the curtain, and dropped down heavily on the bench.

"You expected something like this," said Myrrha.

"No. No, I did not. I thought..."

"You thought what? That you two were on the verge of reaching an accord?"

"Myrrha," he sighed, just a bit annoyed.

"Sorry. I'm sorry. I don't like to see you disappointed."

"We should see to those ingots."

She shook her head. "They won't be in place for eight more days now. There's no rush." She gestured at the envelope. "What does she say?"

"I'm not sure I want to know."

"March..."

He opened the envelope. The note inside had been printed by hand in dark blue ink, with a care to the shape of the letters. He wondered when she had written it; certainly she had not been in a hurry.

He read aloud. "This is my battle. Thank you for your help. Within the day I shall deposit ten thousand thalers into your account. Hoya, PofI." Quashing his annoyance, he refolded the note and placed it back in the envelope, and gave the envelope to Myrrha. "Yet she claims not to have access to her account."

"She said 'deposit,' not 'transfer.' Anyone can make a cash deposit, and she undoubtedly has that aboard her 'skip. Plus a new Palmetto, which would give her access to her bank."

"I don't care *how* she does it, Myrrha," he said testily.

She reached over the table and chucked him on the shoulder. "Then let's just get out of here."

They got.

\* \* \*

"How could this happen?" demanded Thormin Isaora. The Duke of the Isaora Family, he was grizzled and barrel-chested, and had actually fought in battles in his youth, during the brief civil war between cousins that ultimately placed him on the throne. His size and bulk demanded carefully-crafted attire, but at the moment he was wearing a silk dressing gown in cream and silver, having been interrupted at his toilet. He folded his arms across his chest and glared at his son. "Well?" he pressed.

"She attacked me for no reason, sire," said Alexor. Pain from the wound in his arm stabbed at him, and he moaned. "No reason. I didn't do anything, and she cut me for no reason!"

Isaora started to reach out to his son in sympathy, but held back. "You've been cautioned to leave the staff alone," he said, without rancor. "If you have to, go to one of the villages. Thanks to you, we've lost a good cook."

"I'll find her," snarled Alexor. "I'll find her. And when I do…"

"You'd better let that arm heal first."

"It stings! She put something on the knife to make it sting. It hurts!"

Isaora turned to Cajtab, his majordomo. "See my son to his room," he instructed. "I want him to stay quiet and get some rest."

"It will be done, sire."

Isaora watched them leave, the taller majordomo, and Alexor, who never had grown as tall as he had hoped —in more ways than one. His lips tightened, and he shook his head. Of late he had had misgivings about his son's early investment. There had been no other option but his cousin Pathor, who had never received the training he would need, and in any case was of a temperament ill-suited for leadership.

Alone now with his wife Argona in the drawing room, he turned to her. "I fear for our Family," he said, in a hollow voice. "And I confess that I am at a loss."

Argona moved to the heavy brown curtains and drew them open. Sunlight cascaded in from the west. Thormin watched it bestow golden highlights on her fine yellow hair, and thought once again of why he had been drawn to her all those years ago. Almost as tall as himself, she had remained willowy despite giving birth to three, of whom only Alexor remained, the other two lost in the civil war. Although Argona was still of child-bearing age, she had asked to be relieved of that royal duty, and he had granted her wish, as he always granted her wish.

She continued to stand before the window as if she were well aware of his thoughts at the moment, of his memories of her, how he saw her then and now. With a smile of sly mischief on her lips she walked toward him in that graceful way that had first enraptured him at their very first encounter. Reaching him, she placed her hands on his chest.

"I know what you are thinking, my liege," she said to him, her voice the merest whisper of breeze over fragrant grass. "I hereby retract my wish regarding my royal duty."

\* \* \*

Catalina was unable to recall the last time she had spent a day in the sunlight. There was always training to absorb and rituals to be practiced, for a Duchess must always behave just so in public. A single slip, a *faux pas*, might embarrass the Family, or worse, be misinterpreted, with effects that could not be calculated. Of late she had grown weary of this regimen, and longed to step outside, by herself.

So I shall do so, she thought, and garbed herself accordingly. Clad now in a short green kirtle, trousers of brown leather, and sturdy boots, she sent for Tarsha, her lady-in-waiting, and broached her transportation requirement. Not long afterwards, Snarrel Goodling rapped at her door and was given permission to enter.

He was courteous and deferential, and spoke with great care. "May I ask what Milady has in mind?"

"We should think that would be obvious," she replied, silently blaming Tarsha for reporting her plans to him. For betraying her. "We wish to see outside the castle."

He sniffed the air in the room, and frowned, but dared not remark at this time. Instead, he said, "But an airfoil, Milady…"

The airfoil, she thought. Not Tarsha, then, but the groundskeeper. She moved away from the mirror in which she was examining her appearance. "We are quite capable of piloting it, as well you know, having had me taught."

"But alone, Milady," he protested. "At least allow me to send Satrin with you."

Satrin Hommer is your man, she thought. I am for once tired of your people around me, controlling my every move. "We think not, Majordomo."

"May I then ask where you will go, Milady?"

She flashed an easy smile. "But that is the whole point, Majordomo. We do not know where we wish to go. We wish simply to go."

"Then...when will you return? In case anyone should ask," Goodling added quickly.

But who would ask? she thought. "Before dark, we should suppose. If later, the bowlamp will suffice to guide us. In any event, should the need arise, we shall have our Palmetto with us." She looked at him expectantly, the dismissal implicit.

Goodling bowed from the waist. "Yes, of course, Milady," he said, and backed out of the room.

Catalina waited a few more minutes, then left the room and took the lift down to the ground floor. The green airfoil with the silver trim was waiting as she had requested, the fan blades set on idle. She climbed aboard, studied the instrumentation console for a moment, and revved the power. The airfoil lifted from the flagstone paving and obeyed her firm but gentle hand.

Already the castle gates were open, and soon she was flying over rolling grass-covered terrain. The air was fresh and warm, and redolent with the scent of wildflowers. Wind swept her long flame-orange hair over her shoulders and across her eyes. She reduced speed, and took a green headband from a pouch at her hip, and slipped it on to hold her hair in place. Before reaccelerating, she looked around, and decided to head west, toward the sea, and the lulling waves that might bring peace to her.

Hillocks topped with trees invited her, and for no reason at all she downdocked on one of them, there simply to take in her surroundings. To the west, her general direction of travel, lay the boundary hedgerow of Wanderby, and beyond that the sea and some fishing villages, none of which she had ever visited. East, behind her, the castle awaited her return. To the north and south spread more rolling grassland, and in the south an escarpment lifted by an ancient fracture in the crust. She concluded that her choice of direction had been optimal: go where there is something to see.

Perhaps one of the villages would prove interesting.

# 009: Of Flights

In his quarters, Majordomo Goodling fumed. Catalina, his protégée, was developing an attitude that could hamper his plans. Yet there was no immediate help for it. For reasons at which he could scarcely guess, Catalina had begun to exert her independence. Worse, she outranked him, a status she had begun to recognize. Goodling knew the process: tell someone they are good or bad or smart or stupid, and eventually they come to believe it. And he had assured her that one day she would be Duchess of Palologa.

He resisted the urge to hurl a teacup across the room.

And that faintest of aromas in her room; that was coffee, a beverage forbidden to her. If the Duke or Duchess found out she was drinking it, there would be questions he could not answer. Tea, she was supposed to drink tea. He would have to find a more attractive tea blend, to make her forget coffee.

The knock at his door was not unexpected; he had sent for Hommer. He bade him enter.

Dressed in his brown harlequin outfit and belled cap, Hommer stood just in front of the closed door. He belabored the obvious. "You sent for me, Majordomo?"

"What word is there of the *Zelena*?"

Hommer shook his head. "She has disappeared, Majordomo. We have attempted to trace her by her original transponder signal, but that seems to have been changed. The call sign on the 'skip's computer has also been changed."

Goodling considered. "That suggests she is engaged in illegal activity," he said, rubbing his chin as he began pacing the room, muttering to himself. "Why would a princess who can have almost anything she wants become a criminal? What could she possibly gain?"

"If I might suggest, sire?" Hommer said hesitantly.

Goodling glared at him briefly, and relented. The minion was known to have a good idea now and then. "Go ahead."

"Perhaps she was bored, Majordomo."

The notion smacked Goodling, and a question arose: was Hommer speaking of Hoya or Catalina?

"That's an interesting observation, Satrin," he said. It never hurt to compliment even the most useless individual once in a while. "I shall give it some thought. Meanwhile, if you would resume your search for the *Zelena*?"

Hommer bowed. "Of course, sire."

\* \* \*

Afterwards, they lay together naked on the berth, Myrrha along March's left flank, one knee bent across his thighs. His left arm around her shoulders placed that hand on the softness of her breast, though for the moment there was nothing erotic about the contact. The top sheet had been drawn back up over them. Their respiration had become regular again, their heartrates slowed to normal. The conversation of the contact between flesh and flesh made words redundant. The breathless gasps and cries of several minutes earlier made reassurance unnecessary, for there was no doubt it was good for both of them. March basked in the gentle rise and fall of her chest as she breathed.

Remarkable, he thought, that Myrrha breathed at all, for she had no need of air, of oxygen. Nor did her heart need to pump blood throughout her body. These affectations she had created just for him. Such gifts had never before been bestowed by one being on another.

Finally Myrrha sighed. "I hope I don't get pregnant."

March's entire body froze. "*What?*" For a moment, he sputtered. "Can you? I mean, you know...can you?"

"For the hundredth time, March, I'm human. I have ova, you have those wiggly things. It's a good match." She shifted position a little, more on top of his chest now and gazed down into his eyes. "But no; I have control over ovulation. And I would not activate my ovaries without your consent."

"My, aren't we clinical."

"If you wish, I can think of some interesting if vulgar words to describe what we just did."

"What did we do?" he asked blithely.

"Oh, so soon they forget. I'm surprised you don't fall asleep right afterwards. Most men do, or so I've heard."

"I'll try not to snore."

"I know how to keep you awake. Are you up for another?" She ducked her head under the top sheet. "Hmm. No, not yet. Maybe you need some incentive." A few seconds later, she said, "Ah, there we are."

"Myrrha..."

She drew her head back. "So it's no, then?"

"Well...it's yes, but..."

She kissed the tip of his nose. "Having empty-minded thoughts, are you?"

His lips puffed as he exhaled. "Images. Wanderings. The feel of you against me. The way your hair tumbles over your eyes. I love you more than the ingots, you know. If you said let's abandon them, I would. But you wouldn't say that. What else?" He thought back. "Maybe...I don't like that we were misled by someone we went out of our way to help."

She nodded. "I thought so."

"You'd be surprised what enters an empty mind."

"Mine is never empty," she said.

"I suppose a part of you was solving differential equations while we were connected."

"Connected? March, we were making love," she said severely. "And no, I don't find differential equations particularly stimulating...hmm. Although perhaps in the throes, instead of 'goddesses, *now*!' I could try crying out, y-prime equals the sine of x."

"That's a simple one," said March.

"We were making simple love. Next time let's try for y triple prime plus x times y-prime minus four x-y equals zero."

"But I'm not suicidal. How about something in between?"

She rolled on top of him, straddling him, and perforce he entered her. "I thought you'd never ask," she breathed.

* * *

Presently Catalina came upon a river that looped the land like a discarded ribbon. As it appeared to flow toward the sea, she decided to follow it, keeping well to the right bank. She was unable to recall being this close to a river before. It soon struck her that the outer portion of the loop was undercutting the bank, while the inner consisted of a sand bar deposited there by the current. She had received an education, but nothing about this. She knew where the forks and knives went in relation to the plate, and she knew the difference between a perfunctory greeting and a genuine expression. But where did the water come from, and what lived in it?

She felt as if she had lost something that she had never known she possessed.

With her progress toward the sea, the castle dwindled aft, while above the horizon a rag of white cloud scudded across the sky. Catalina felt as if she were abandoning one world for another. In the distance ahead stood the stretch of low hills that marked the westernmost boundary of Wanderby. Beyond it lay nameless coast, peppered by small villages. So much topography she had been taught; now she was seeing it pass under her fan blades. Hovering above that coast, red-orange Solntsa prepared to bed down for the night. She rather imagined that when it sank below the sea she would hear a hiss.

Her request keyed into the instrumentation console elicited the response that she had two more hours of daylight remaining. At Palologa Castle, dinner was almost over. She checked her Palmetto for messages; no one was concerned for her, or made remark about her absence. Probably Goodling had covered for her, saying she was indisposed and had already taken a light meal.

Two more hours.

She was loathe to turn back, but the choices were clear: stay somewhere for the night, or return to the castle. Only after she turned the airfoil around did she realize that she had not considered that she was returning home.

\* \* \*

In Room 7 on the upper level of *The Parsley Sprig*, Kamie Isaora sat on the bed and gazing out the window into the night. She had found some clothing that almost fit; Garla's daughter was about half a forearm shorter than Kamie's meter-seventy-five, but equally as slender. Moreover, the boots and shoes in the closet alcove were close enough to her size that if she rubbed hand soap on her feet each day, the tightness would not cause blisters. At the moment, however, she was less concerned about attire. Jinzy had not responded to her Palm.

Kamie had sent three messages so far. At this time of night, Jinzy should have been in her room, preparing for the next day. It was possible that she had been caught up with the second kitchen shift until she was assigned a new partner, but Kamie was unable to quell the bleak sense of foreboding that had draped itself like a shroud over her shoulders.

Almost ready to give up, she Palmed Jinzy one last time. Seconds passed, and she was about to abandon the attempt when Jinzy's bruised and battered face appeared in the screen.

Kamie's heart thudded. "Jinzy, what happened?" she gasped.

The tip of the girl's tongue moistened split lips. "Where...where are you?"

"Never mind that. Jinzy, what...?"

"I-I tried...tried...your bed was still made, I-I..."

"Tell me," Kamie urged, softer.

"Alexor," she said hoarsely.

Jinzy's left green eye was closed, with purple all around it, especially on the cheekbone. The right eye was better, but half-lidded and swollen. Kamie counted more bruises on her chin, and her nose was a mess, the right nostril still trailing a thin streak of blood. Jinzy's disheveled brown hair covered half her forehead and partially obscured the lidded left eye. What Kamie could see of her neck showed bruises that might have been caused by an attempted strangulation.

Kamie's heart bled; guilt and shame colored and heated her face.

"He kept asking me where you were," said the girl. "Where, and then he'd hit me. Where, and then he'd hit me again. I thought it would never end. I didn't know what to tell him. I didn't know where you were."

"I'm so sorry, Jinzy."

She looked down. "It's not your fault."

"Yes, it is. I should have warned you. He...tried something with me, and got his arm cut open for it."

"But you got away, then," Jinzy said, with faint cheer. "That's good."

"Jinzy, you have to get away, too."

"I-I can't. How can I?"

"Just like I did. Start walking. Pack what you can carry, and start walking."

"I'm scared. And it's dark."

"Then go to the Palologa Family. It's only half an hour's walk away. They'll protect you."

Jinzy shook her head. "I-I don't know..."

"You have to do something," Kamie said firmly. "You have to get out of there."

"I know...Kamie, can you come get me?"

"I don't know. Maybe. Look, go to Palologa now. Tonight. If I can figure a way to come for you, I will. And I'll stay in touch. Palm me when you get to Palologa."

"All...all right."

"Pack. Go. Then Palm me."

"I-I will."

Kamie closed out. A string of vile words escaped her, most of them directed at herself. I have to make this right, she thought. Whatever it costs, I have to make this right. I have to fix this.

# 010: Life's Questions

After leaving *The Locker*, Hoya went directly to the private hangars at Grenadine Spaceport, unlocked her *Zelena*, and climbed aboard. The feeling of home overwhelmed her immediately, and for a long time she sat in the starboard captain's chairs, arms and legs akimbo, a sponge to the atmosphere and familiarity around her. Many difficulties lay ahead, and they needed to be considered, but she thought that she should not consider them, not now. They could wait. Wanderby was not going anywhere, and neither was whoever had attacked her. The sauerbraten settled in, easily digested, and soon she fell asleep.

By the time Hoya awoke, night had poured itself onto this longitude of Grenadine. She had not thought herself so exhausted. She had caught a few hours of sleep in the guest stateroom aboard the *Bluebolt* while they were traveling, but it had not made up for the nights on Calla Cried. Even now, she yawned and stretched and considered trudging aft to her stateroom to finish off the night.

But there was something in her diary that had made people seek it, and destroy her two cottages to find it, something that was critical to her ascendancy. She had no idea what it could possibly be, and doubted she would recognize it when she perused the pages she had written. At length she stood up and went to one of the upper bins in the bulkhead, and retrieved the leather-bound book in which she had recorded the events of her life from the time she could write to the time she had been marooned. Minutes later, fortified with a mug of Viridian black tea, she sat down again in the captain's chair to read.

An hour and another mug later Hoya had finished reading the diary without having found anything that stood out as a rationale for the tribulations she had suffered. The entries were typical—immature at first, for she had begun the diary when she was five, then on to pages whose margins were adorned with flowers she had drawn, and toward adolescence some notes on what she thought was important, though it were mundane. The last four years' pages were written in a neat hand in dark blue ink, and chronicled her studies and her subsequent activities. While some of those activities were of interest to various authorities, none was related to her royal status.

Nothing, in short, was making sense.

Still, by the time she had finished reading, she had come to the conclusion that the Palologa majordomo, Snarrel Goodling, was not always to be trusted. There was nothing she could point to and say, "Aha!" But intuition told her that he'd had a purpose behind his purpose when he had sent her away to school.

Hoya got up and stretched her limbs again. "Procne," she said, addressing the 'skipcomp, "take us up and enTrack us for the night."

Instantly the Videx was filled with the matte black of null-space. *"It is done, as you see."*

"Yes, thank you." She headed aft. "Wake me at sunrise, please." Assuming, she said to herself, I can get any sleep at all.

In a half-dream, Hoya screamed to the goddesses to get her off Calla Cried. In her heart she knew this was impossible, because until March had come to rescue her, she'd had no idea which world she was on. She came half-awake blinking, the echoes of that scream dying in her ears. Only partially did she sit up before sleep began to recapture her; she rolled over to face the bulkhead. It walled out the rest of the Universe. She fell into a fuller sleep while wondering what she had been dreaming about.

The constant laughter of a fine silver bell awoke Hoya. Still tired, she swung her feet to the deck and sat up, woozy. A hand to her head steadied her. "All right, Procne, you can shut it off now."

The tinkling stopped. *"Do you have a course you wish me to set?"*

"Procne, I don't know what I want right now. I don't know where I want to go or what I want to do. No, belay that. I want to see my parents. But it must be done…"

*"Gingerly?"*

"As good a word as any. And not just yet."

*"Hassan twice tried to reach you during the night here. I told him you were indisposed. He left no messages."*

She stood up, and divested herself of clothing. "Tell the Guildmaster I am not interested," she said, drawing on a fresh reseda outsuit. "Was there anything else?"

*"The comestibles are almost outdated. You should go shopping."*

"Taken under advisement." Hoya made for the bridge. "I think I want breakfast," she said, passing along the gangway. "There's a quiet café in Ballyrushes, right next to a fromagerie and salumeria. Set course and enTrack, please."

*"On our way. May I ask?"*

"Of course, Procne."

*"We are bound for Ravensnest. Is that because it is on the way to Faedra?"*

Hoya reached the bridge and sat down, grinning. "Why, Procne, whatever do you mean?"

*"I thought so. Arrival in forty-eight minutes. Shall I make a reservation?"*

"No…yes! Under my name." She went directly to a bulkhead bin and took out a Post Sizzler, ejecting the charge packet before testing the play in the enable button. "Let's find out if anyone is looking for us."

\* \* \*

Alexor heard the kitchen door open and close, and quickly dashed to a window to find out who had gone out so late at night. Spotting a shadow of movement, he waited until it passed through the dim light from the window. He recognized Jinzy immediately. The urge fell upon him to bring her back and question her again. But she was carrying a backpack and a rucksack. Clearly she did not intend to come back. He crept out the door to follow her.

Minutes later it became clear to Alexor that Jinzy was headed for the Palologa castle. It seemed unlikely to him that Kamie had taken refuge there, so Jinzy's visit could mean but one thing: that she expected Kamie to come for her. The very thought of revenge brought a snarl of fury to his lips. All he had to do was find an ideal vantage point, where he could cover all approaches to the castle, and wait.

Wait, and he could take them both down. One for the knife slash, the other for lying. A corner tower of Isaora Castle would afford the best view. Meanwhile, he continued to follow Jinzy to verify her destination. Despite the fragrant scent of night bloomers and the twinkle of points of light in the sky, he was motivated by the heady aroma of a girl's fear and pain that trailed from the scullery maid back to him. From a hundred paces away, he saw light appear in a doorway at the rear of Palologa Castle. One of the scullery maids—Hallia, he thought it was—had opened the door for her.

After the door closed, he made for the tower to begin his vigil. He sensed that Jinzy had been told to seek refuge in Palologa. The only person who could, and would, have told her that was Kamie Isaora. Alexor had no doubt that he would see her soon enough. His heart leapt in anticipation.

\* \* \*

A heavy heart kept Kamie Isaora awake for much of the night, until finally exhaustion overtook her. She had received a Palm from Jinzy that Hallia had taken her in for the night, but that was small comfort as she tossed and turned. The Palmetto sounded the alarm much too early, or so she thought. Dawn was already pouring light through her window—she had been too tired to draw the curtains.

Eagerness to start the new job gradually overrode her lack of sleep. Quickly she prepared for work and went downstairs. A faint aroma of drink and tobacco still hung in the air, but the windows and doors had already been opened and fresh air filtered in, bringing with it a whiff of salt and brine from the sea. Garla was moving tables around—patrons always rearranged them during their visits, said the barkeeper—and Kamie assisted her in this. It was physical labor, as the tables were sturdy and seemed to resist this intrusion into their lives. When the rearrangement was complete, Garla bade her stop.

"You didn't sleep well." It was more concern than accusation.

"I'll be all right."

"You know, I don't even know your name."

"It's Kamie."

"Kamie..."

She hesitated. "Just Kamie. What's next?"

"Dishes and metalware out of the washer. They go into cupboards and drawers behind the counter."

Kamie moved into position, while Garla went into the kitchen to fire up the grill. They spoke through the ready window where the prepared orders were put up. During this, Garla asked or hinted at questions, until Kamie finally started talking. At first the words came hard for Kamie, for she had yet to prove her worth at work, and by disclosing her personal problems she was risking her room and her job. But Garla was listening with a barkeeper's ear. The more she listened, the more Kamie talked. Unnerved by the unexpected sympathy, she revealed everything that had transpired the day and evening before. Throughout it all, although she was crying, work continued.

More preparation followed—rows of mugs straightened, the counter wiped, the coffee brewers set up, the floor swept with a stiff broom. An hour or so later they caught a break, and sat down at a table with mugs of coffee.

"You're doing great so far," said Garla, hoisting her mug. "Basically we want the place clean and neat, service provided as promptly as possible, I'm sure you've practiced that where you were."

Kamie nodded. "Tried to. Sometimes people are hard to please."

"We hardly get any people like that here. Maybe once in a while a fisherfolk who's had one too many might raise his voice, but there are others around him to settle him down."

"How do we order supplies?" asked Kamie.

"As needed. I'll show you in a few days." Garla straightened on the bench. "Which reminds me, we're low on eggs. We usually pick up four dozen at a time. You go seaward to the first cross glideway, turn left, and the dairy farm is about five kilometers along."

"You want me to go get them?"

"If you would, please."

"All right. Do I pay for them, or what?"

"We have an account there."

Kamie started to rise. "I'd better get started, then. That's a bit of a walk."

"Can you handle an airfoil?" asked Garla.

"I've gone solo before."

"There's a white and gold one out back. Use that."

"Thank you."

"And Kamie...I don't expect you back for five hours."

Her eyes teared up as she suddenly understood. "Oh, goddesses," she breathed.

"Go. Shoo. I'll finish up here. Go get your friend. But don't forget the eggs."

\* \* \*

Restless, Newcombe March wandered onto the bridge with a plate of rolls, butter, dried fruit, and cheese. He had already showered, and was waiting for Myrrha to finish hers. The restlessness stemmed from Myrrha's remark earlier about becoming pregnant. It had not been presented in the form of a gentle nudge or hint regarding their relationship, but as a simple statement of fact. But it had begun to grate on him. What did he want? What did she want? He was in virgin territory here, for no man had ever, as far as he knew, taken up with his 'skipcomp.

Even as that unique situation occurred to him, he knew he was approaching it from the wrong perspective. Time and again, Myrrha had assured him that she was human—something of a hybrid of computer and flesh, but a fully functional human being, for all that. He ought to adjust his thinking. During the two years that Myrrha had been with him, he'd had other women, usually for more than a night. The relationships had not endured because at heart he was still a rogue, a pirate, and a smuggler, and therefore not the sort of man with whom a woman might build a lasting relationship.

So what was Myrrha?

The question was too heavy for him, but before he could dismiss it, Myrrha arrived on the bridge. She was still green, and attired in a lime green outsuit and dark green loafers, and she smelled faintly of lilac soap. All her allurements were engaged as she sat down on the port captain's chair.

March made a show of sniffing the air.

"I thought you might approve of the scent," she said, and looked over his plate. "Is that the last of the cheese?"

"I'm afraid so," he said, and offered her a chunk of smoked gouda.

She took a roll as well, and cut it open and buttered it. As she started to take a bite, she noticed he was watching her. "You *have* seen me eat before," she said.

March averted his eyes. "Sorry."

"You're still mulling over how I could be able to become pregnant," she said, with just a note of accusation in her tone. "You still aren't seeing me as a woman, not entirely."

"It's not that," he said. "Well, maybe a little, but... Myrrha, I don't know what I want."

"You can have other women."

"That's not quite what I was alluding to."

She chewed thoughtfully. "You mean, you and I, and where are we going?"

"Something like that. Myrrha...do you truly want a child? Children?"

"No, not...not yet."

"When, then?"

She made a face and shook her head. "It's not that simple. Let me ask you this, and bear in mind that the computer aspect of me knows the answer. How much money do you have in your account with the Bank of Relay?"

March laughed. "I thought you kept track of that, so I wouldn't have to."

"As I thought: you don't really know."

"Tell me."

"Just over forty-seven million thalers."

The figure shocked him. "Seriously."

"How much is enough, March? How much more do you want?"

Still nonplussed, he shrugged. "I-I hadn't actually set a goal. Smuggling and a bit of hijacking is what I do, along with some odd jobs on contract."

"Illegal activities all."

March sighed, and closed his eyes. "For years, on and off, before I met you, I wondered how I had come to be in this business. I even had a couple sessions with a hypnotherapist who regressed me. I came to understand myself. Whenever I did something wrong as a child, I was not punished for my transgressions, but beaten. After a while, I learned, not right from wrong, but not to get caught." He opened his eyes again. "And I don't get caught."

"March...maybe it's time to do something else, you and I."

Again he laughed. "All right. What?"

"That, my love, is for you to decide. Meanwhile, we're almost out of cheese."

"And how do we solve that problem?"

"Ravensnest isn't that far. There's a great fromagerie and salumeria in Ballyrushes."

"I know. *Fromagerie Les Alpages*. We've been there before."

"Shall I set course, then?"

"Myrrha..."

She made a show of batting her eyelashes at him. "Yes?"

Words failed him. He wanted to say something, and had no idea what it might be. Finally he settled on, "Yes, set a course for Ravensnest."

# 011: Intersectionality

As soon as Kamie became familiar with the airfoil's controls, she set a course directly for Palologa Castle and engaged the autopilot. That done, she Palmed Jinzy, desperately awaiting a response. When it came, she saw that Jinzy's face was still swollen, but the injuries had been treated.

Alarm showed in her green eyes, the brown flecks in them stilled. "I think I was followed here," she said, her voice creaky.

"Alexor?"

"I can't think who else it might be. Where are you? The background looks like an airfoil."

Kamie considered the matter. If Jinzy had been followed, that could only mean that Alexor had the castle under surveillance. It also meant that he might be watching for her to come for Jinzy.

"Wait one," she told Jinzy, and began rummaging around in the storage compartments. Disappointment set in when she was unable to find any weapons, or anything that might serve as a weapon. She muttered an imprecation she seldom used, and returned to the Palmetto on the instrumentation console.

"Almost certainly he's watching to see what you'll do, and he's probably expecting me to show up. He's evil, but he's not stupid. He's sly."

"So what do I do?" asked the girl.

"Are you packed?" Jinzy nodded. "Stay ready by the back door to the kitchen. If it opens, like for deliveries, stay well away so he can't see you."

"I don't know where he is."

"There's a grove of shagbark trees about two hundred paces away. He may be lurking in it. That's all right. I left on foot; he's not expecting me to come back by airfoil. Here's what you do."

\* \* \*

Hommer seldom availed himself of the little cubicle that served as his office. Poorly appointed, it had a desk and a straight back wooden chair with no cushion, and a thin curtain that allowed sunlight to shine directly into his face from dawn to midday. The walls were plain white, as was the ceiling, into which had been set a cross of five illuminative panels. The hardwood floor had never known a carpet. He worked in the office whenever absolutely necessary, because it afforded him a measure of privacy, allowing him to monitor events and maintain communications on the Palmetto without anyone looking over his shoulder.

At the moment, the Palmetto on his desktop was conducting a search for various keywords, especially *Zelena*, for Hoya Palologa would surely seek out her spaceskip now that she had escaped from Calla Cried. The device was also monitoring communications traffic for anything related to the woman or the 'skip. So far, however, Hommer had received no notifications.

He was about to begin his breakfast when a beep sounded from the Palmetto. Curlew in Interstellar Communications had detected a hit on *Zelena*. The 'skip had just docked down on Ravensworld.

With shaking fingertips he keyed a quick message to Snarrel Goodling and requested instructions.

The response contained not a word of compliment for his efforts. Instead, the words were stark and clear: Send an armed team. Abduct her. Space her body near a star.

Hommer sent messages to assemble the men on Ravensworld. Six, he thought, should be more than enough to take down a simple princess.

\* \* \*

Unlike other worlds sparsely settled by humans, Ravensworld had a large and vibrant population, with cities, towns, and villages scattered over three of the four major landmasses, all in the temperate zones. One of the earliest to be exploited after the invention of Track had enabled humanity to travel anywhere in the spiral arm in no more than a few hours, it had developed an independent and self-sufficient economy and industry, exporting far more than it imported. As most of its products harked back to old Earth, it was a landing zone for the nostalgic tourist as well as for temporary visitors. Tall buildings and sprawling suburbs typified cities, while the towns and villages knew a rustic atmosphere.

Ballyrushes, located on the west coast of the continent of Galileo (the other two settled continents were Newton and Hawking), resembled one of the smaller port villages of the British isles. Served by a modest spaceport, it was best described as tranquil. Although the residents lived and worked as folk had done for millennia, visitors found the idle appearance relaxing. One might sit on a patio outside a shop and sip beverages and consume local fare all day and accomplish nothing more than relaxation.

Hoya Palologa, however, had business to transact inside the restaurant *Chez Nous*, whose front windows gave onto a view of the bay along which rested Ballyrushes. She had come for breakfast, but also to place an order to be filled by someone on the restaurant staff at the adjoining shops. A small table with a view of the door and the front windows and a chair with its back to the wall suited her needs. She placed an order for tea and currant scones, and another for various items from the shops next door, paid with her reactivated fundscard, and sat back to await service and deliveries.

In the meantime there were the aromas of baked goods to savor, intermittent traffic to watch, and soft shadows moving in the park across the glideway as the sun rose in the sky. Soothed by the moment, quiet minutes passed, and Hoya almost failed to notice the arrival of her breakfast. The tea was superb—she had always favored the darker blends—and the two triangular scones were fresh-baked. She ate and sipped while she considered her next steps.

In the past nine years or so, making contact with her parents had failed on every occasion. Even the few messages she had sent had gone unanswered. As she would have been notified in the event of their...well, she did not want to think about that. She tried to tell herself that they were busy, but how busy could they be? In any event, she needed to get in touch with someone who could update her on doings in the castle.

And she had to be careful about it. While certain that Kamie did not betray her, someone had been lurking about for her. Perhaps a Palm was overheard? That made sense, but who would have been interested in her contact with Kamie?

Who else, who else?

That girl, a friend of Kamie's. Jindy? No, Jinzy. Hoya checked her list of Palm contacts without finding the name. Still, Procne could trace the girl. She sent a Palm text to the 'skipcomp with that instruction.

Hoya poured a second cup of tea, happy for the idle moments. Patrons came and went. A couple of men entered and looked around, but with scarcely a glance in her direction. Nevertheless, her senses went on full alert. Neither man appeared to be the type that would order tea and scones. Hard faces, grizzled and scarred, dominated by hard eyes. One man wiry, his taller companion burly, and both attired in casual, loose-fitting clothing and soft-soled shoes. Their attention soon focused on the displays of baked goods.

Hoya didn't believe it for a second.

When a third such man entered the *Chez Nous*, and two more came into view on the far side of the glideway, she suspended belief altogether.

\* \* \*

The news from Hommer had roused Snarrel Goodling from his sleep, and left him wide awake.

Anticipating now the final disposal of Hoya Palologa, he paced his bedroom, thinking, thinking. The next step in his project was ready to implement, but he had to wait for confirmation of her abduction and demise. He felt no sense of urgency. Aside from the untimely escape of a young woman who was supposed to have died, and the unexpected willful behavior of Catalina Palologa, matters were proceeding according to the rough sequence he had planned. There were always right moments in any strategy, great or small, and to rush those moments invited failure or even disaster. No, he had to wait for news. In the meantime, there was preparation to be done.

Finished with attiring himself for the day, Goodling entered his adjoining office, placed a breakfast order, and sat down at his uncluttered desk. One matter needed a reconciliation: the difficulty posed by Catalina's independent streak. It was not totally unexpected, for she was a healthy young woman with hardly anything to do. Hommer had been insightful in referring to her as bored. Perhaps it might be best to look the other way. Willful or not, she would die soon enough.

Breakfast arrived in the hands of Hallia, who placed the tray at the edge of his desk and backed away. But he noticed that she had picked up the butter knife and held it for longer than necessary in order to place it just so beside the little platter of bread rolls. He kept a bland expression to cover the pleasure of knowing that she was emotionally and spiritually incapable of harming him, regardless of provocation. As she was moving the knife, he reached out to her hand and gently extracted it from her, before selecting a roll and buttering it. Liberated from its tiny burden, her hand trembled. For a moment he considered using her now, but he had a schedule of tasks set for this day, and Hommer was likely to Palm him at any moment with news.

"I'll see you after dinner," Goodling told her in dismissal. He felt the urge to celebrate. "Plan on spending the night."

Meekly Hallia inclined her head in acknowledgement, added a perfunctory, "Yes, sire," and eased herself from the office. The door made hardly a sound as it closed.

Alone, Goodling gazed pensively at the Palmetto on his desk. After he finished the first roll, he tokked the device. A few seconds later, the pale face of Clewthe Neerdawell, majordomo of the Lascora Family, came into view in the screen, his dark eyes as always furtively darting this way and that, as if to assure himself that he was not going to be overheard.

"Is it time?" asked Neerdawell, his eyes not quite meeting Goodling's.

"Almost. We need to review and adjust the final steps. And bring that fresh trake fish you promised. I may want to arrange dinner for the duke tomorrow evening or the next. Come see me before then. Use the middle entry, and don't disarrange my clothes when you come through the closet."

"I've said I was sorry about that. What time?"

"I'm awaiting news. Make it midday. Use a servants' airfoil, and dock it in our servants' lot."

Neerdawell was aghast. "Really, Snarrel."

"This is no time to arouse suspicions. And dress appropriately."

Scowling, Neerdawell closed out with no further words.

Goodling's lips pursed as he watched the face of the Lascora majordomo fade from view, and once again he wondered how much he could rely on Neerdawell. A heavy sigh settled him. He tokked to send a text to the Guildmaster, not to withdraw the contract, but to stand by. But there came a return text stating that Marzanna was not interested in any offers at the moment. Goodling frowned as he considered alternatives, should the need arise. Who else was totally reliable? It was not a question he could ask the Guildmaster, and risk insulting him.

He glanced at the time on the Palmetto. "Where are you, Hommer?" he growled, and leaned back in the chair. He had waited years for the next several days to come; a few minutes here and there meant nothing.

# 012: Strategies and Fruition

The airfoil, already traveling too fast, could not go fast enough to suit Kamie. A headwind from the east gave the craft moments of turbulence. After a particularly bad jostling that almost caused her to lose control momentarily, she reluctantly decelerated to a safer speed. Frustration tried to set in, but she shook it off. Rescuing Jinzy was her only concern.

She reviewed the overall plan and found a vulnerability. She was approaching Palologa Castle from the east. If Alexor was watching—and surely he had the castle under surveillance—he would observe that she had come from the east. Almost before her brain gave the order, her hands at the controls swung the craft to the north, so that she might arrive from that direction, or misdirection, as she now thought of it. She also meant to depart toward the north. The journey back and forth would take longer, but leave them safer.

She fretted anyway.

Five kilometers, Kamie decided. A straight-line approach from the north to the rear of the castle, and the same distance back to the north before she altered course to the west. Envisioning kept her mind active, and drew the focus away from her anxieties and fears. Eyes straight ahead, she told herself, as she now turned back to the south. This is it. Five more minutes.

At three minutes out she was able to discern the shape of the castle, an architectural relic of the distant past, and to distinguish its superfluous battlements. Iron bars protected the lower windows, but created the illusion of a trap. A trap that she was about to spring.

One minute. She tokked the Palmetto on the console. Jinzy responded right away. "Where are you?"

"About half a minute out. Stay on with me. When I tell you to come out, toss your things aft and climb aboard."

"He's out there at the trees." Her eyes were wet with tears of fear, and her voice quaked. "I *saw* him. Kamie..."

The rear of the castle loomed before her, "Take a deep breath. He can't run two hundred paces fast enough. Almost there."

Even as she spoke, Alexor emerged from the grove, his right forearm bandaged. Ignoring him, she scudded to a halt at the back door of the castle. "Now, Jinzy!" she yelled.

But two girls emerged running: one was Jinzy; the other was short and sturdy, yellow-haired, and attired in drab kitchen garb. A girl whom Kamie belatedly recognized as Hallia. Each cast two laundry bags onto the airfoil.

Incoherent, Alexor was screaming furiously as he dashed to catch them.

Kamie reached for Jinzy's hand and tugged her aboard. Hallia struggled to climb up, and finally tumbled over the side and spilled into the aft bay just as Alexor reached the airfoil. He leapt against it, the impact rocking the airfoil. He hung onto the top rail even as Kamie turned the airfoil around and tried to speed away. The additional weight of Alexor caused the airfoil to roll, and she was barely in control. Flashes of movement out of the corner of her eye said that Jinzy was slamming one of her laundry bags against Alexor's hands. Something heavy and ceramic shattered inside the bag. Alexor screamed, and fell away. Kamie wrested control back and sped off. Vile words from behind rang in her ears.

"I'll find all of you! I'll find you and kill you!"

\* \* \*

"Hmm," muttered Myrrha.

She was sitting in the port captain's chair and gazing at her Palmetto lying on top of the instrumentation console and the recording that played in its screen. Already forgotten was the mug of water that March had brought her, so focused was her attention on the device. Again and again she tokked to rerun the recording.

March, sprawled and half-dozing in the starboard chair, finally came fully awake, driven by curiosity. "Something?" he asked her.

"I'm...not certain."

He sighed. "Okay, what are you doing?"

"It's the recording of the investment ceremony of Hoya Catalina Palologa."

"We've seen it."

"But we haven't examined it. March...come and look."

He eased himself from the chair and crossed the bridge. She moved the Palmetto to where he was able to see it clearly and paused the recording.

"Who do you see?" she asked.

"Hoya, age thirteen. She looks a little different now, but that's her."

Myrrha's eyes narrowed. "I agree. But watch what happens when I zoom on her face."

"It's still Hoya," he said.

"Look closer."

"I am. I see Hoya." He frowned. "I don't understand what you're getting at."

She sat back and looked up at him. "Think back. She's thirteen. She's been gone for four years, attending school. What happened to her in the interval?"

"I-I don't..."

"Her nose was broken, March."

"As it shows in this recording, Myrrha."

"Right. Right. But by her own statement, she was always at school. She never returned for her investment."

"Maybe she forgot...okay, wait."

"No, she is most unlikely to have forgotten her investment. Conclusions, please?"

March examined the stilled image again. Nothing he did, now that he realized the truth, could make that young woman back into the one he and Myrrha had known for two days.

"That girl there is not Hoya."

"*Précisement, mon amour.* Yet it looks like her, *even to the broken nose.* Which she broke at age ten, while she was away at school."

"So we're looking at a substitute," March said slowly, trying to think around the impossible. "Someone whose nose was deliberately broken in order to match that of the real Hoya."

Myrrha nodded solemnly. "And the real question now is: how did they know the real Hoya's nose had been broken?"

"Gods and goddesses," breathed March, as realization set in.

"Indeed. They've been watching her all along. At least up to the time she went on to university."

"They being?"

"It's not her parents," said Myrrha. "You can see them standing by, in fine raiment, pleased by the ceremony. They think she's Hoya."

"It could still be her parents."

"March, they would have no motive to invest a look-alike to the throne. But someone else might."

"Snarrel Goodling."

Her head bobbed, nodding. "Sure as the goddesses made little green apricots."

"Apples. Little green apples."

"I've always had a bit of a blind spot with apples." She flashed a grin, and grew serious. "March...this also explains why her parents haven't been in touch with her. *They don't think she's gone.* As far as they know, she's lived there at the castle since she was invested."

"And this is why Hoya was marooned on uninhabited Calla Cried and expected to die there without anyone finding out," added March. "They can't murder her outright because that would risk leaving signs of assassination, and implicate Goodling. They have to disappear her."

"March, we have to find her. We have to help her, because right now we're the only ones who can."

\*   \*   \*

Kamie flew the airfoil well to the north before she banked to the west. The castle was but a tiny block in the distance, but she was alert to pursuit. Beside her on the bridge stood Jinzy and Hallia. The wind had dried Jinzy's tears, but left her brown hair in disarray. Every few seconds she ran her fingers through it in a futile attempt to keep it out of her eyes. After a while, she gave it up.

Her voice was hoarse when she finally spoke. "I-I don't know how to...to..."

"I had to come for you, Jinzy. I had to. I'm so sorry. I should have known he would..."

Her words trailed off as Jinzy laid a hand on her arm. "It doesn't matter now," she said. "It's been written. It's done. You came for me."

Kamie set the autopilot, braced her arms on the console, and let out a long sigh. "*We* did it," she breathed. "Hallia, you weren't...but I suppose you have your reasons."

"One very large reason," said the girl, but looked downcast. "I'm sorry if this...inconveniences you."

"Not at all. But you could explain it to me on the way, so I know what I'm getting myself into."

Jinzy squeezed Kamie's arm. Her grateful expression morphed into one of concern. "Where are we going? And where did you get this airfoil?" A scary thought occurred to her. Eyes wide, she asked, "You didn't steal it, did you?"

Kamie laughed. "No," she replied, and explained how she came to be flying it.

"Then you got a place to stay, and you found work," said Jinzy, amazed.

"So do you, maybe both of you, if you want to work there."

Jinzy's smile came easily, despite the bruises. "You and I have been working together for twelve years now, ever since I was six. I'd hate to lose a good thing."

Kamie was silent for a moment. "Was that the vase you made that I heard shatter?"

Not a note of regret touched Jinzy's tone. "It was in a good cause."

"Garla needs help," she went on. "I'm sure she'll take you on. You can room with me." She took a long moment to examine the two girls. Finally she said, very gently, "You two don't have to be afraid anymore. Go aft to that bench and sit down, relax. We have another hour before we reach Carrikdove. There are blankets in the bins. Use one for a pillow, and cover yourselves. You're safe now. You can sleep without being afraid."

Jinzy almost wept as she headed aft. "That will be a new experience," she sighed. Hallia followed, holding her head up now.

\*   \*   \*

After docking the *Bluebolt* on the tarmac at Ballyrushes Spaceport, March and Myrrha took public transportation—an old-fashioned self-propelled conveyance—and rode with seven other passengers to the town center. The journey took them past tranquil parks, a pond with colorful waterfowl, a field where children played incomprehensible games according to adjustable rules, and several people sitting on benches in the shade, reading or talking. The overall atmosphere had its attractions, but March was not certain that he was ready for a more sedate life. Prolonged idleness did not become him. A glance at Myrrha told him that her thoughts paralleled his. Ballyrushes was a good place to visit, to shop, but was not a place that he could see them living.

"Something more," said Myrrha, reading him. "Quiet moments are good in moderation, but we're doers, not sitters."

He started; she had found words for what he was thinking. He took her hand, and they twined fingers, and watched the town wrap itself around them.

The *Fromagerie des Alpages* stood as they remembered it. In essence an overgrown kiosk, it differed from other shops in that it had a vast cellar, where cheeses and wines continued to be aged after they were delivered from vintners and curers. An adjoining subterranean room was reserved for sausage and deli meat processing. March and Myrrha had taken the obligatory tour a year earlier, and had fallen in love with the place.

The conveyance dropped them off, but on the far side of the glideway, where a bazaar was underway. Enthused, Myrrha grabbed his hand and yanked him toward it. Almost immediately they were overwhelmed by a potpourri of aromas and odors. Costermongers awaited by their carts, tending the coals in their small firepits and frying various foods on demand. Hawkers cried out their wares. The smell of new leather, the remnants of its soap and oils, hitched rides on a light breeze. Perfumes, sampled on wrists, escaped. March caught a whiff of machine oil as they drew near a display of tools. Relatively few people were wandering about, for the bazaar had just opened. For the moment, hawkers outnumbered the traffic.

"Are we looking for anything in particular?" March asked.

Myrrha demurred. "I just like to look. Thigh boots of leather might be nice, if I found something to go with it. A short tunic or kirtle, perhaps, to show off my thighs."

"I thought you 'created' the garments you wear."

"I also like actual clothes." She started to move on, but March was fixed in place. "Something?" she asked.

He was studying a pair of men who stood at the perimeter of the bazaar, watching the café across the glideway. He did not respond immediately to her question. Presently he came away with her.

"Not sure," he told her. "I thought I recognized someone."

"One of those men? Dressed for labor, both armed?"

He stopped, laughing. "You saw that?"

She kissed his shoulder. "I learned from the best. So who do you think he is?"

They moved on, stopping at a table display of jewelry. Myrrha picked up a fine silver chain with an ivory cameo on jade pendant.

"I know him under the name Faragan Boiche," March answered. "Heavy hitter. Freelance."

"The one with the droopy mustache?"

"He started out with a gang called Temmen, but they kicked him out for improprieties."

Myrrha frowned. "A criminal gang with proprieties? That's refreshing."

"They try not to hurt people, but Boiche likes it. But it might not be him. Do you want that necklace?"

Her voice was the merest whisper, the words to herself but just loud enough for him to hear. "Next thing I know, he'll want to see me wearing this and nothing else."

"How much?" March asked the hawker.

"Two hundred thalers," she replied.

"One-fifty."

"Split it?"

"Done," said March.

But before he could pass her the fundscard, a hard buffet of displaced air knocked him, Myrrha, and the hawker off their feet, and blue beams from an energy weapon lit the air outside the café.

# 013: Sea Changes

Intuition told Hoya that the men inside the café were reluctant to make a move until they got her out to the glideway. Already she had undone the top of the cargo pocket on the right thigh of her outsuit, where the Sizzler rested. With the Palmetto flat on her table, she surreptitiously tokked it, raising Procne, and quietly keyed a clear and crisp instruction. Even as she finished, a shadow loomed over the table. She looked up, an auburn eyebrow raised in a question, and found the wiry man before her. His right hand was hidden under his shirt.

"Nobody in here has to get hurt," he said, his voice deeper than she might expect.

Hoya did not move. "I had no idea people like you were concerned about bystanders," she said blandly.

"We're not. But you are. Let's not make this difficult."

She sighed in resignation, and got to her feet, left hand holding the Palmetto. "Lead the way," she said, and noted that the other two men were blocking any retreat.

They eased from the café onto the boardwalk that fronted it. As she walked, Hoya's right hand swung back and forth over the open pocket as if in the natural rhythm of her steps. As the wiry man signaled to a nearby airfoil, she spoke one word, very softly. "Procne."

In a split second, on the grassy easement between the glideway and the bazaar, a great egg the color of freshly-sheared copper materialized out of null-space on four support pods. Its appearance squashed the two men waiting for Hoya. Prepared for the burst of air, she remained on her feet and braced against the door jamb of the café, but the three men around her, and bystanders, lost their balance. She drew the Sizzler and fired three precise beams. Two of her adversaries managed to fire their own weapons, but in the act of dying, the beams went aloft. Around her, people screamed and shouted, while she dashed toward the *Zelena*.

Myrrha was first to recover, and pulled March back to his feet. Previous experience told him what had happened, but even so he looked with amazement toward the spaceskip that had just downdocked on the glideway easement. He also spotted someone running. Unable to credit what his eyes were telling him, he started running toward her, and finally shouted, "Hoya!"

Hearing her name, Hoya turned toward the sound and fired a blue beam at him, but it passed easily over his head and dissipated. By that time, she was already clambering up the ramp and through the open hatchway. In the conditions of a quick security lockdown, the ramp retracted and the hatch sealed. A burst of air—toward the *Zelena* this time—spilled March to the grass as the 'skip dematerialized back into null-space.

Again Myrrha yanked March to his feet. "Track her!" he ordered. "Get that transponder ID!"
"I did not wait for you to say I might," she told him. "I have it."
Still shaken, he looked around, and pointed. "That empty spot beyond the bazaar," he told her. "Remote the *Bluebolt* there, and let's get out of here."

\* \* \*

Bleak black images filled the mind of Alexor Isaora as he fumed in his bedroom, nursing three broken fingers on his left hand. At first, upon returning to Isaora Castle after his unsuccessful attempt to intercept Kamie, he had stalked into one of the drawing rooms, only to find out that it was occupied by his father the Duke, who cast him a hard frown. Alexor had then retreated to a secure room where he could vent. The more he considered the matter, the angrier he grew. Kamie was just a common scullery maid. She had no right to refuse him, and certainly no right to attack him the way she did. All he wanted was a look, just a look. And a feel. The lure of warm available flesh was irresistible, and the mere thought of it aroused him.

And that other kitchen quiff, Jinzy. He'd had his eye on her for some time, savoring the anticipation of taking her. Of all the young female kitchen workers in Isaora Castle, only those two and one other had remained aloof to his hints and suggested advances.

And what was that Palologa kitchen quiff Hallia doing there? No matter, no matter. By all the gods, he'd show them all. He would find them and show them.

An airfoil. How did Kamie get an airfoil? He knew she would come for Jinzy, but on foot, not in an airfoil. Where had she gotten it? Stolen it, probably. That's what the kitchen staff did; they were all thieves. His father couldn't see it, but he could, and when he became duke, then by the gods he would...

But where did she get the airfoil?

He thought back. White with gold trim it was, and a standard model. In his mind's eye he could see it clearly now. But its origin could not be identified by its colors. Still, there was something on the port quarter. A smear of green. Maybe it was related to the ownership of the airfoil. A symbol of some kind. Kamie Isaora had stolen it somewhere.

He laughed bitterly at her name. She was not even Isaoran.

His fingers ached. The pain medication the family doctor had given him was not working. He swore venomously, recalling the unprovoked attack and the cracking of his finger bones.

Green. In his memory he squinted at the smear, to bring it into focus. He saw it, at first without understanding what he saw, for it made no sense to be there. A cutting from a very leafy plant. It had to mean something.

Maybe the majordomo would know. Cajtab knew everything that went on, and said nothing about it, unless asked. He meant to ask.

\* \* \*

Hommer spent the first several minutes in a shock that was almost catatonic. Impossible that she could have escaped, impossible! And five hardened men dead as she made her escape, even more impossible. But the airfoil pilot who had witnessed the carnage was insistent. And now Hoya was gone, lost to him. What was he going to tell Goodling? What *could* he tell him?

Slowly Hommer's thoughts turned to flight. If he remained in the castle, the failure could well cost him his life. But where was he to go? Goodling would send others to find him, and they would not be gentle, bringing him back to meet his fate.

The entire situation was *impossible.*

In the end, after considerable wringing of his mental hands, Hommer concluded that he had no choice but to report the failure, and hope for a lesser response than the one he anticipated. He was not out of options in this matter, because he had never had any to start with. Trembling fingers raised Goodling on the Palmetto.

"Impossible!" was Goodling's comment, after Hommer completed his report. His face in the Palmetto reddened.

"Sire..."

"No, Hommer, I accept the witness statement. But you hired on six men, each of whom had killed at least one person, am I right?"

"Yes, sire."

"But they weren't professionals, were they?" It was not a question. "They were violent men who had killed during the course of their lives."

Just a little, Hommer began to relax. "That's correct, sire."

Goodling sighed. "I should have insisted on a professional. All right, Hommer, I'm not pleased by the failure, but you did your part. I'll have to resolve this myself. Meanwhile, see if you can find out what's going on at Isaora. I hear talk that two of their kitchen staff have run away. This suggests instability of leadership, something that I can ill afford now."

"I will find out, sire."

In his office, Goodling scowled at the Universe. How hard could it be to kill one princess? But now he had no choice except to ask the Guildmaster to try again with Marzanna. Hiring the assassin entailed the risk of exposure of Hoya Palologa's death as having come from hire, but he was out of options now. He would double the contract price, even triple it. He understood the assassin's reticence, of course. Marzanna was reputed to be very selective about his contracts. He had to have a reason before taking one on; the target had to be a miscreant of some sort, someone who should be shoved out the airlock. A princess, in his eyes, would be an unlikely candidate. Still, thought the majordomo, if the money was right, anyone would abandon their principles.

He raised the Guildmaster once again.

\* \* \*

"She's in null-space," said Myrrha. "I can detect her transponder when she deTracks, but that's no guarantee that we can catch her up."

March understood; the *Zelena* could well depart again before they could reach her point of detection. He began to wonder whether they should abandon the chase. It had been painfully obvious even before this latest encounter that Hoya did not want their help. He had to ask himself now whether he was being unreasonably persistent and stubborn. As a man he had always accepted a no from a woman, albeit mostly in matters of interpersonal relationships. Why could he not accept rejection from Hoya Palologa?

"I can tell you why," said Myrrha.

He flopped down in the starboard captain's chair and sprawled. "Go ahead," he said wearily.

She eased across the bridge to him and knelt down on the deck beside the chair. Laying her head against his knee, she gazed up at him.

"Because at some point in your life, even though you learned not to get caught, you also acquired a certain moral sense," she said, her voice as gentle as a light rain. "Gradually you developed a view of right and wrong. You decide *ad hoc* which is which, rather than base the decision on a set of principles. But you do in fact choose, and apart from your work, I've not seen you choose the wrong. It's one of the reasons why I love you so much: you have an innate goodness, despite your childhood and despite what you do—what *we* do—for a living."

He had to smile. "Myrrha, I'm not so sure I can live up to you."

"But you try, my love. You do try. And I am with you always."

For a long moment he thought about that. A sea change was in the wind, and he chuckled at the mixed metaphor. But where would the waves or the wind take him? Of a certainty the destination lay in uncharted territory. In ancient times, such territory was listed as "there be dragons here." Still, he had faced dangers before, when he was alone. Now Myrrha...

His eyes regained a bit of focus from his distant thoughts, and once again he looked at her face. Oval face, very pale green skin peppered with dark green freckles. Luminescent deep green eyes that looked at him and through him, and sometimes on out to the rest of the Universe. He could but guess at the thoughts and notions behind them. He and she were mysteries to one another, and yet she knew so much of him, reluctant though he was to admit it. And she herself was...was...

The completion of that thought left him stunned. Realization set in. He understood now what she had been telling him all along. He knew now, for certain and for sure, who she was.

"Thank you," she whispered, before he could speak, and lightly kissed his knee.

"For?"

"I can see it in your eyes. You now think of me as a woman."

"It's...more than that, Myrrha. But..."

She quirked an eyebrow. "But?"

"I-I don't know if I want to be a father. I don't want to raise a child the way I was raised. I don't want the child—or the children—to become what I became."

"They won't. We'll work together, like we have been. I'm already me," she said. "And you have not been that other person for a long time. You're you, too."

He released a shaky sigh. "I think...I think I want to go back to Ravensnest," he said. "And buy you that necklace."

"I want to wear it for you."

"Better set a course, then."

She grinned. "Already done. We'll be at the bazaar in an hour and a half." Her eyes flashed mischief. "Whatever shall we do while we wait?"

# 014: Twists and Turns

In retrospect, Hoya wondered whether she should have fired at March. But he had been so inquisitive, so searching for answers from her that she was unwilling to give. In time she had told him part of the truth, but not *the* part. In any event, he had found her. That meant he had been searching for her. Basic lesson in staying alive: there are no coincidences. So if he was searching for her, it could only mean that he was in the employ of those who wanted her dead.

Yet she was not sorry that she had missed him. Perhaps her brain, against her purpose, had told her hand something. The shot was easy—less than ten meters. She could not have missed; yet she had done.

At length Hoya drew herself away from those thoughts. Whatever had happened, was now written, immutable. Only the future required pen and ink. She decided to peruse her diary once more for answers.

Meanwhile, she had set no course. It was safe here, lurking about in null-space. Here there was no "here," for mathematically she and the 'skip had a quantum probability of zero. No one could find her, or even detect her. But eventually she would have to downdock. Where, where?

A ping from the communications monitor on the bridge roused her. "Procne, who is it?"

*"Guildmaster Hassan."*

"Tell him I'm not...no, belay that. Put him on. I'll tell him myself."

The familiar mustachioed and goateed face of Malik Hassan appeared in the monitor. His head was bare, and his dark hair was as usual in disarray. Piercing dark eyes transfixed Hoya, but she was well aware that the Guildmaster had no other expression. He spoke in a low and even voice, slightly accented.

"You have been difficult to contact."

Hoya gave a careless shrug. "I've been busy. And I'm not interested in any contracts at the moment, Malik. I thought that was made clear to you."

"The client is insistent. He wants you. He's willing to pay triple your rate."

That astounded her. "That sounds desperate," she said, after a quiet few seconds. "Desperate clients can be unpredictable and unreliable."

"Thus the payment in advance. But this client is one you've served twice before. Apparently he likes your work."

Hoya wondered who it was. But Guild rules forbade him to reveal the name—she herself was anonymous except for her code name. "How soon would I have to do this, Malik?"

"The day before yesterday."

"That bad?"

"I gather there is some urgency. He did not tell me what it was, nor could I have asked."

She sighed resignation. "I suppose I can spare a day or two. Who is this malefactor?"

For the first time, Hassan looked distressed. "Initially I was reluctant to consider receiving the contract, Marzanna, as it's not your usual fare. The target does not meet your precondition of someone who should be shoved out the airlock. So far as is known, she hasn't committed any crimes or offenses. Apparently she is just in the way; the client gave only vague details in that regard. And you have to locate her first, which may present a problem."

"She? I'm to kill a woman?"

"Her name is Hoya Catalina Palologa, of Faedra. She's a—"

"Wait. Procne, block visual."

The peremptory command filled the bridge. She sat back, her expression one of extreme disbelief and incredulity. Questions raced furiously through her mind, and she felt the onset of a headache. What, what, what? And were her parents in danger? Concern and dread seeped into her psyche. Her hands trembled. The lights in the overhead seemed to be dimming. Recognizing the vulnerability of her agitation, she drew a few meditative breaths to restore her self-control.

At least she now could surmise the identity of the client. That gave her an advantage she might exploit. But the irony of it all, the irony!

"Procne, enable visual. Hassan, I accept the contract." Because if I take it on, no one else will, she added silently, and I won't have to keep looking over my shoulder. "Is there any other information you can give me?"

"She was last known to be at a café on Ravensnest, but is not there now. One hundred fifty thousand thalers are being deposited into your account even as we speak. The other half on completion, as always."

She drew a long breath and slowly exhaled. "Understood. I'll be in touch. Procne, close commo."

Alone again on the bridge, she burst into laughter. Snarrel Goodling unwittingly was paying her three hundred thousand thalers to commit suicide. She got up and went aft to the galley, and debated for a minute or two whether to eat something or settle for a mug of tea. In the end, she opted for the latter; nothing helped like tea to settle her mind. And she now had much to think about.

*     *     *

Kamie brought the eggs in through the back door of *The Parsley Sprig*, followed by Jinzy and Hallia. Garla's immediate reaction was of sympathy. Although she was in the middle of the midday meals, she went back into the bay and announced to the patrons that she needed to deal with a situation and that there would be a fifteen-minute break in service. She then returned to the storage room where the girls were waiting, got out the first-aid kit, and treated Jinzy's bruises. Finished, she leaned back against a stack of canned goods.

"You both worked in kitchens?" she asked. The girls nodded. "As I told Kamie, there's not much money, but the food and the room are comp. How are you for clothing?"

They held up their laundry bags. "We have a few items in here, but...but not much," said Jinzy.

Garla sighed. "Well, there are some items in Kamie's room that might fit you. Meanwhile...well, first, do you two want to work for the tavern?"

They nodded emphatically.

"We finally have a full complement of staff," she breathed to herself. "All right, then. I'll advance you some wages. There's a pre-worn apparel shop a little further seaward on this side of the glideway, called *Worn Again*. You should be able to find something that fits. You'll need shoes with slipless soles; grease and oil sometimes slick the kitchen floor. You're all rooming in Seven. Kamie, get a third bed from Five this evening, along with the linens and pillow." She dug into an apron pocket and withdrew a clutch of silvers. She counted them as she distributed them. "Off you go. Come in through the back door when you're done. Kamie...you've got ale to draw and serve. Let's get back to work."

Minutes later, on the boardwalk that sided the glideway, Jinzy and Hallia were basking in their good fortune. They cringed inwardly at the first few passers-by, until they became accustomed to the friendly nods of greeting. Kamie's assurance that the girls would be safe and welcome in Carrikdove was proving out. Hallia sighed relief as they sat down on a bench for a brief rest.

"It's not like you expected?" asked Jinzy.

"In the castle, we are what we are, and will always be," Hallia replied. "Here it's early days yet, but already it feels like you and I, strangers, are part of a community. I-

I can't quite explain it yet, how I feel. I'm not...Jinzy, I'm not scared anymore. I'm away from the majordomo, and I'm safe. Or safe enough, anyway."

Jinzy looked away. "I've heard how Goodling... treated you."

"I think you broke Alexor's fingers."

"I was aiming for his head."

They both laughed.

"Garla reminds me of my mother," said Hallia. "Before she...died."

Jinzy rapped knuckles on Hallia's knee. "Then we'd better buy some clothes and get to work for her," she said, looking seaward as she pulled Hallia to her feet. "The sign is two shops down.

\* \* \*

The relaxed mood of Snarrel Goodling gradually faded with the sky at dusk. Already he had filed away the matter of Hoya Palologa; with Marzanna on her trail, the princess was as good as dead. But another Palologa female was missing, she from his room, for he had distinctly ordered Hallia to come to him following her duties. It was possible, if annoying, that the girl was still seeing to her kitchen duties. He resolved to find out in a few minutes.

Meanwhile, there was the matter of the visit from Clewthe Neerdawell of Lascora Family the next day. Neerdawell had a useful hobby: his interest in toxins. It was he who had provided the tetrodotoxin years ago when first one son and then another were born to Justinio and Olena Palologa. The poison, derived from a fish known only on Earth, had no antidote, and best of all, no one on Faedra recognized the symptoms.

But where was that kitchen quiff Hallia?

Goodling rang down to the kitchen, and learned that she had not shown up for her after-midday shift. He ordered a runner sent to her quarters. Several minutes later the runner informed him that she was not within.

Eager to be helpful, the youngster said that he had heard she had run away.

Goodling collapsed onto a stuffed chair, the first premonition of plans gone awry now looking at him as if wondering where to begin gnawing at him. Hallia gone. She was the key to the coming phase of his strategy. When the Duke died, she would be blamed. But unless he could find her...

He tokked his Palmetto for Satrin Hommer, and as always, the response was immediate. "What are you doing now?" he asked the minion.

"Sire, I am considering that the diary you seek is aboard the *Zelena*," Hommer replied. "The castle's Interstellar Communications post is listening for mention of—"

"Never mind that now," the majordomo snapped tersely. "Hallia has disappeared, apparently run away. Have her found and brought straight to me."

"At once, sire."

"Someone must have seen her leave. Inquire around. Offer silver, if that seems useful. But find her!" He closed out without waiting for Hommer's acknowledgement.

\* \* \*

"You appear to be deep in thought, my liege," said Olena Palologa.

Justinio nodded absently. "I thought tomorrow to take a walk with Catalina," he said, his tone vague. "I fear I have been neglecting her. Try as I might, I cannot recall a single quiet moment she and I have shared, though I'm certain there must have been some."

"We have neglected her, you mean." She sat down beside him on the divan, moving cushions around until she was comfortable. "The majordomo has done well with her, but perhaps our part in her training could have been increased. And I think that a walk with her is a good idea. Or perhaps a ride in an airfoil. I heard yesterday that she had taken one out, though goddesses know where she was going."

"Perhaps she wished to see more of the holding she would rule one day." Even the air he exhaled sounded tired. "It is well that she is taking an interest in it."

"Or she is looking for a consort," offered Olena.

He laughed. "She won't find a proper one out there."

She studied his face, a fond expression on hers. "There might be someone of the proper lineage," she said quietly. "Oh, my liege, I've always known of your few early dalliances, while you adapted to life with me. Yet here you are, with me. It's quite all right."

Justinio felt his face warm, but only a little. Time since then had well passed. He fell back into thought. "We haven't exhausted the possibilities at the Lascora Family. Catalina has shown no enthusiasm for Pathor, but there are two brothers..." His voice trailed off as he looked to Olena for a helpful and supportive comment.

"Neither has reached his majority, my liege."

"But they will one day. This is about the future."

She reached out to touch his arm. "She is nowhere near the age where she will succeed you, my liege. Give her time."

"The majordomo has her somewhat in thrall."

"It has been so ever since she returned from school for her investment. I wonder...perhaps she went out on the airfoil just to get away from him for a while."

A note of disbelief crept into his tone. "Why, I do think I am looking forward to this," he whispered.

"As you should do, my liege. As you should do."

\* \* \*

Jinzy wanted to work the evening shift, giving Hallia the rest of the night off. As her first service, carrying a three-ale order that Kamie had taken, she took the mugs with some nervousness to the designated table and placed them one by one in front of the patrons. These were garbed as fisherfolk, all not much older than she, and she felt herself on edge, wondering what they would say to her. Shocked she was to hear expressions of gratitude, for rarely in her years of food service at the castle had anyone thanked her. Slowly she walked away, with a glance back over her shoulder, and wondered what sort of place the tavern and all of Carrikdove would prove to be.

The men at the table drank and talked and laughed, and Jinzy and Kamie took and delivered various orders, while Garla did most of the food preparation. This was by design, for she wanted to observe the two while they worked. People came and went, including the trio to which Jinzy had first delivered ales. When she went to clear that table, she found three silvers and two bronzes in a neat stack by the empty mugs. She took the coins to Garla, explained where they had come from, and asked her to register them in the cash bin.

"No, those are yours," said Garla, as she turned over a pair of fish cakes for sandwiches. "They're your tip."

That staggered Jinzy's thoughts. "My...my what?"

"Your gratuity. They thought you provided them good service, so they left a little note of gratitude for you. They tipped you."

"I-I...goddesses." She regained her voice, and dropped the coins into a pocket of her apron. "Is this... does this happen often?"

With deft and practiced moves Garla dressed a pair of fish sandwiches and set them on a plate. "These go to table four, please. And yes, it happens often enough."

What is this place? Jinzy silently asked herself, as she headed for the table. Why are people so kind? I don't deserve—

"Easy with that plate," said Kamie, passing her. "Are you all right?"

"I-I don't know. Just…it's a different world here, Kamie. People say please and thank you, not 'where's my food and hurry up.'"

"We can talk about it after work," said Kamie, and moved off.

The two men who received the sandwiches hungrily took first bites and nodded approval. The younger of the two—Jinzy thought he might be around her age, which was eighteen—was looking at her face. "What happened to you?" he asked her.

In no way anticipating such a question, Jinzy had no ready answer for him. Aware that she had to respond, she finally managed a, "It was a bad situation."

"Well, I hope it got fixed."

She decided she liked his smile. The recollection of her vase breaking made a brief appearance, adding to that smile. "It did that," she said.

She turned away, but he said, "I see Garla hasn't passed out a name strip for your apron yet."

"I'm Jinzy."

"I hope that's a name and not a description. I'm Caber."

She repeated his name, and walked away, astonished to find herself laughing.

The evening sped on, and quieted down. Jinzy began clearing tables for the night, including the one where Caber had sat. There, she found two silvers on top of a folded piece of scrap paper. She opened it and read, "I'm happy to have met you. C."

After a moment, and a pair of wet eyes, she tucked the note and the coins into her apron pocket.

# 015: Darkness and Dawn

Goodling awoke to the faint hint of sunlight that seeped through gauzy curtains, not having heard back from Hommer regarding the missing Hallia. Until she returned, or he had found a replacement, the strategy was on hold. After checking to see whether messages had been left to him, he prepared himself for the day.

As he headed for his office, the Palmetto in his pocket pinged. In the screen he saw the face of Turpren, the junior groundskeeper. Goodling needed no interruptions. "What is it?" he snapped.

"I thought you should know, sire. Lady Catalina is taking out the airfoil shortly."

Another annoyance! "Thank you," he replied, and started to close out.

"The Duke is going with her."

Goodling paused. He was uncertain what this signified, but knew that it did not bode well. If he was losing control...he had terminated the prolonged application of a mild statin that induced memory loss and enabled the insertion of new memories. It was just possible that Catalina was recovering far more quickly than was predicted. If she should experience a trigger...a person, place, or thing, it might undo some, or even all, of the work he had done on her.

He heaved vile words into the air as he trudged into his office. Only a few more days did he need, and then it would be all over. With Duke Justinio dead, followed by Catalina shortly after her coronation, and with Neerdawell doing his part with the Lascoran royal family, the two houses would be able to overwhelm Isaora and unite all of Wanderby. Unite with himself as the head of all three houses.

But...Hallia gone. And now a growing independence in Catalina. Time, he needed time, and he had no way to manufacture it. Hoya's diary sank to secondary importance, for it would only signify during the transition period from Justinio to Catalina. Hoya would not be able to stake a legitimate claim to the throne, being dead. In a few days, no one could oppose him.

In a few days.

In the meantime, there were still tasks of a majordomo nature to perform. The kitchen might need supplies. So might the cleaning staff. Groundskeepers and transportation, and communication, all fell within his purview. He made a show of appearing now and then, but relied on section chiefs to provide him with updates as needed. His own position was supervisory: the chiefs provided him their requests, and he signed off on those of which he approved. Menial, menial. He was tired of it. He deserved better.

On a corner of his desk Goodling perched a heavy hip. With the status of Hallia now uncertain, he needed another diversion, as well as an unwitting replacement to serve Duke Justinio his last dinner. There were but a few possibilities: servile, even cowed, yes, but young as well. He matched names with physical appearances and came up with two options—Cinya from the kitchen, and Desshelle, who trimmed hedges and tended the roses that Olena Palologa loved so much. But Desshelle was proficient with the clippers, loved the outdoors, and might prove contrary. He made a mental note to have Cinya pay him a visit later today.

The Palmetto on his desk signaled an incoming message from Hommer. Immediately Goodling knew the news was negative, the minion being reluctant to face him. He turned the device so that he could read it. "Hallia said to leave on airfoil with Isaorans Jinzy and Kamie. Destination unknown."

He started to slam his fist down on the Palmetto, and only at the last second did he catch himself from destroying the device.

\* \* \*

The encounter Alexor desired took place in the hallway on his way to the dining hall for breakfast. Cajtab, the tall and thin and saturnine majordomo of the Isaoran Family, was making his rounds among those staff who served on the second shift. As was his custom, Cajtab said nothing by word or look until the royal family member acknowledged his presence.

That done, Alexor said, "I wonder whether you can help me, Majordomo. Somewhere I saw a symbol, or perhaps an emblem, that I cannot identify and cannot get out of my head. It is most troubling."

"Perhaps if sire can describe it."

"Oh, yes, of course. It is green, and I-I don't know...it looks rather like a cutting from a leafy plant. Hmm...I believe I can recall seeing it on the bow of an airfoil. Perhaps a delivery to the castle? I am uncertain." He peered up at Cajtab's long and drawn face. "Does it remind you of anything?"

"Nothing immediately comes to mind, sire," said the majordomo. "However, I can tell you that, given it was as you recollect on an airfoil, it was not one belonging to any of the Families. A delivery, perhaps, as you suggest. However, I will make inquiries. Perhaps someone else has seen such a craft and knows from whence it came."

"Please tell me as soon as you find out anything," urged Alexor. "This whole thing is beginning to drive me spare."

"Of course, sire."

"So far, so good," mumbled Alexor, as he sauntered on toward the dining hall.

\* \* \*

Kamie awoke to the sound of tears nearby. "Lights five percent," she ordered, and saw that Jinzy was sitting on the edge of her bed, elbows aprop knees, head supported between her hands. "Hey," said Kamie, as she swung her feet to the floor and sat up.

"Hey," murmured Jinzy.

"Bad dream?"

"What?" Her voice shook. "Oh...no. No, I just...oh, goddesses, I don't know how to..."

By the last quivering word Kamie was seated beside Jinzy. "After all these years, you can't talk to me?" she said softly to the girl.

Jinzy almost laughed, despite the tears. She reached for the apron, now draped over the foot of the bed, and took a folded piece of paper from a pocket. This she handed to Kamie without a word.

Kamie opened it and read, then folded it and returned it. "C for?" she asked.

"His name is Caber."

"And he has made you sad."

"What? Oh, no, no. I am not sad. I am scared."

"Of him?" said Kamie, frowning deeply. She looked as if she were ready to break something...or someone.

"Of...of me."

"I'm listening, Jinzy."

"It's...no man has ever told me this," she said, making a desultory gesture with the note. "I-I want to feel something, but I don't know what to feel."

"What do you want to do about it?"

"But what *should* I do about it?" Jinzy shot back.

"Well...he didn't ask to see you. He didn't say he would be back. I think the next move is up to him, and then it's up to you."

"But what if he...he's...you know. Like...like *him*?" Through clenched jaws she grated the last word, then won back her worry. "I mean...he sounds good, he looks...nice, he's...I think he's fisherfolk."

"An honest occupation."

A tiny smile found its way to the corners of her mouth. "He did smell a little of fish."

"That can be washed off," said Kamie. After a moment, she added, "So can the past."

"If I give it a chance. I know, I know. But what if...?"

"You're saying 'what if' as if it were necessarily negative. But Jinzy, what if it's positive? Isn't it worth taking a chance to find out?"

For a long moment Jinzy considered that. "So if he comes back to the tavern...?"

"Be yourself. And if he ever gives you his heart, try not to break it."

Now she laughed. "I will. And I won't."

Kamie got up. "I'm going back to sleep. Try not to snore."

"I don't snore!"

"Yes, you do," said Hallia.

\* \* \*

Worry kept Hoya from sleeping. She tried a bottle of red wine, and only succeeded in later wobbling from the bridge to her stateroom and issuing an incoherent instruction to Procne, who duly ignored it, having seen her like this before. Stretched out on the berth, Hoya felt her head begin to swim. That, or the stateroom was rotating. Still, the problems confronting her now were clear enough. Her parents were in danger. She was being hunted, albeit by herself. Something was seriously amiss in the Palologa Family. And she was drunk. Inebriation could be slept off, if one could sleep. But the other factors...

Music, she thought. Aloud, she said, "Music."

As always, Procne had been listening. *"Something light classical from the G's, perhaps? Gershwin, Goodman, Grand Funk, Grieg..."*

Words sobered her, just a little. "Vivaldi. Something soft, with a cello."

*"Cello Concerto in E Major?"*

"Please. Procne...I need help. I don't think I can do alone what I have to do."

*"You tried to kill the only ones who were willing to help you."*

"Don't remind me. And anyway, I missed." Vague thoughts scudded across her mind like clouds in a high wind, and she was unable to catch any one of them to focus on. At last she gave up trying to think. "Procne, do you suppose they're still on Ravensworld?'"

*"I'm sure I have no idea."*

"Set course for there and enTrack. Wake me when the bazaar opens. And turn the music down. Cello or not, my head hurts."

\*   \*   \*

The bazaar had been closed for two hours by the time March and Myrrha returned to Ravensworld, and stars were leaking light through the shroud of night. For a time they sat on the easement grass underneath those stars, each with their own thoughts that somehow always seemed to dovetail, neither of them speaking to one another, nor even touching, for their presence together was eloquent as to their developing relationship. At last the night grew chill, and they repaired to the *Bluebolt* and a quick Track to the Ballyrushes Spaceport to dock for the night.

Quietly they made their way to the stateroom they now shared, and to the berth. She watched him methodically undress—boots first, then shirt and trousers and unders. Then in a starwink her own attire vanished. While his eyes took in the entirety of her, her green color motif shifted to pale sienna for the skin, to umber for her hair and eyebrows, and to rich chocolate for her eyes and pubic thatch. He thought this new iteration might be symbolic, for much had grown or changed between them.

They slipped under the top sheet and for a while lay side by side. Finally he spoke.

"The four million thalers that Noyle placed in escrow for the ingots? Would you please transfer them back to him, give him my regrets, and tell him to find someone else?"

"A moment," she said, and a moment later, "It is done."

Presently not a ray of light shone between them, nor could anyone say where one ended and the other began.

In the morning they awoke and delicately untangled themselves, and sat up. Stretching and yawning followed before Myrrha said, "The *Zelena* has deTracked."
"Where is she?"
"Docked alongside us."

# 016: The End Begins

Catalina was already at the airfoil controls and was about to rev the fan blades preparatory to liftoff when Duke Justinio emerged from the rear door of the castle and approached her. She was not unhappy to see him, but puzzled and concerned. Was he about to order her from the airfoil? But his sunlit face seemed pleasant enough, and he even had a smile for her, the first she had seen from him in a while. To her surprise, he actually indicated with his hand a request for permission to come aboard. Though she could not have said why, she readily granted it.

Justinio moved to stand beside her on the bridge, and gave her a second mild shock. "Let's go," he said.

"Sire?"

"Appa," he said. "You used to call me 'Appa,' remember?"

"Oh. Yes, of course."

"Where are we going?"

The question stumped her. She had no particular destination in mind, and with her father aboard, her choices felt limited.

Her words came hesitantly. "Appa...I just wanted to fly about, nothing more than that."

"And we are in *Wander*by."

Catalina laughed, and the airfoil lifted off. On her previous journey she had spent a few pleasant moments atop a hillock with a small cluster of trees, where she had a panoramic view of the landscape for as far as she could see. There had been wildflowers casting their fresh scents to the wind, though at the time she had paid scant attention to them, being more interested in the freedom that the open spaces had accorded her. Now she decided to return to that hillock, to the northwest.

Settling on a destination gave her an opportunity to consider why her father had come aboard, for he had shown little interest in her activities, or even in her. But she dared not ask him why, and spoil the moment. Worse, she felt constrained by his presence, as if now she had to behave just so. Visible at a distance, the leaves on the hillock's trees glistened silver in the sunlight. She pointed toward them, and set a course in that direction.

Soon they passed over a fan of shallow creeks that fed the meandering river, and a field of yellow flowers, most of them in full bloom, the rest waiting for another day or two of sunlight. Catalina once again was reminded of knowledge she did not possess. What fed the creeks? Were they seasonal, dependent upon the spring rains? What lived in them? So focused on these questions that she did not hear one from her father until he repeated it.

"You seem engrossed in the landscape."

She hid a smile. "What about you, Appa? Do you smell the flowers, or hear the waters talk, or see the leaves shine in the sun?"

"You are correct, Hoya."

"Catalina, Appa. Hoya was my childhood name." He did not respond. "Correct in what way?" she asked.

"I should take more flights and more walks."

She raised an auburn eyebrow at him. "And perhaps less croquet?"

He laughed. "I stand rebuked. But your mother loves the game, and I do like to make her happy."

And what about my happiness? she thought, but did not voice the question, for she felt it did not become her.

They reached the hillock. Catalina found a level spot for docking, and set down there. Justinio disembarked first, and offered her a helping hand—a third shock to her system, but one that she accepted after an initial hesitation. They found a spot where enough sunlight filtered through the trees to warm the grass and flowers.

"There are no benches," he said. "It looks like we're standing."

"Oh, Appa," she sighed, and sat down, tugging him by the hand down beside her.

"Aren't there creatures in this grass?" he asked, placing himself delicately on an unfamiliar surface.

"Probably. But they don't bite...much." At her equivocation he shot her a concerned look, and she went on, "We're outdoors, Appa. Of course we have to share the land." Abruptly she pointed. "See there? In the distance, that's the river. I followed it for a while, but the day grew late, and I decided to turn back. I wonder where it flows to. Probably to the sea. I've never seen the sea. I've never seen much of anything except the castle and some of the surrounding grounds."

"Desshelle does fine work tending the roses."

"Yes, she does. I think they bloom for her in gratitude for her care."

"That is a strange thing to say."

"Not at all, Appa. I don't...I haven't studied much except what I was told to study, but there is so much more to life than proper curtseys and knowing the difference between a spoon you eat soup with and one you stir the cof...*tea* with."

"I confess I had not thought of it that way. Catalina, are you suggesting that your education has been incomplete?"

"Worse than that, Appa. It has been focused on my future duties, which are based mostly on rote behaviors. But I want to *think*. I want to *know*. I want to *understand*." A heavy silence followed, during which she scarcely drew breath. "I want to live," she whispered.

"Catalina..."

Still whispering: "I want to drink coffee. I-I..."

"But you like tea," he pointed out.

"I was told to like tea," she groused. Wasn't I? she asked herself.

"The majordomo was assigned to see to your upbringing and education. The same way I was brought up by the previous majordomo."

She smiled. "The previous previous one, I think it was."

"Am I truly that old?"

She leaned her cheek against his arm. "Not at all, Appa," she said affectionately.

Now the silence between them had the substance of warm white clouds. Catalina keened her ears to sounds, something she had not done on her earlier wandering because the whirr of the airfoil blades had blotted out anything she might have heard.

A faint rustling in the grass between them drew her attention. At first, she was unable to discern the cause of it. Gradually a double blade of grass came into near focus; one of the blades was moving. She saw a long and narrow green body with more legs than she could count. It was crawling upwards. She put a fingertip to the upper third of the grass and held it there, waiting for the creature to reach it. At the barest contact with her finger, it drew back the upper half of its body. More tentative attempts at contact followed. Clearly perceiving no harm, the creature began to crawl up her finger. The pointed ends of the legs seemed to tickle her. She watched while it reached the back of her hand, then raised that hand so she could study the creature. It had two eyes, a mouth that closed sideways, and two feelers protruding from the top of its bulbous head.

It occurred to her that her father was watching her intently. She turned her head to look at him. There was something in his gray eyes that she thought of as rapt attention. She guessed that he had never before seen such a creature.

"Is it dangerous?" he asked her.

Her reply came easily, carelessly. "Not so far." She lowered her hand to a clump of wildflowers and allowed the creature to escape onto it. The experience made her shiver, but with a quiet excitement, not a cold chill of relief. How many more wonders awaited her? Surely something lived in the waters. The seas. She looked up. The skies. And what wonders did the stars hold?

"So far away," he said.

"Yes, they are."

"I meant you, Catalina. I watched you. Your thoughts were distant, remote. I cannot imagine where you were."

No, she thought, you cannot. And I am so sorry for you for that.

"It seems we each have our own worlds," he said.

"Yes, Appa. But you are tied to yours by duties you think you cannot escape." You are not allowed to stir your tea with your soup spoon, she added silently.

A moment later, he said, "I think perhaps I should return to the castle."

"Yes, Appa."

\* \* \*

Through the Videx March saw that Hoya was waiting for them. She held no weapons in hand, but there was a telltale bulge in the cargo pocket at her right thigh. It was facile to believe the beams in it were not meant for him and Myrrha. She had fired at him—or at them—the previous day. What would prevent her this day?

Moreover, she was standing with the early sunlight at her back. It might have been inadvertent positioning, or she might have hoped to blind him when he emerged from the 'skip. If the latter, how would a princess know to place herself there for that reason? Even while he watched, she shifted her weight to her right leg, and folded her arms across her chest. Waiting. Impatiently. Her outsuit, he noted, was white, glistening where the light reflected from it. When he reached the bottom of the ramp, she would be almost invisible.

March was aware of Myrrha before he saw her step up beside him. Once again reading him, she said, "So we wait until the sun rises higher."

He did not glance at her. "One day you are going to have to tell me how you do that."

She nuzzled her cheek against the point of his shoulder. "Oh, no, *mon amour*. To do so would violate the code of the women."

"You just made that up."

"Not so! Women always see more than they say, and know more than they reveal. It's in the literature. From Shibiku to Austen and Brontë to Cherryh and McCaffrey to Shellivan and Parsho. They keep their counsels, and reveal something only when their men need delicate and careful advice, or when the women want them to do something without so saying." She shrugged. "It's in the literature."

"You've read all that?"

She laughed. "I only turn pages during foreplay. After that it's...what is that precious old phrase? Katie-bar-the-door?"

He chose to ignore this, especially as he had never heard that phrase before. "Did you brew coffee?"

She handed him a steaming mug. "Of course."

He took a cautious sip, and found the temperature to his liking. He made a little gesture with the cup toward the Videx. "What does your literature say about our girl out there?" he asked.

Myrrha considered. "I think she is who she claims she is, but she is also someone else, and that difference is why she has been so secretive. But she revealed part of that when she fired at you."

"It was uncharacteristic," he conceded.

"Of a princess, yes, but only if we accept the stereotype of a princess. She does not have enough hair to allow her to escape the tower."

"I hope you didn't mix any metaphors into this coffee."

"Just some love, *mon amour*. Just some love. But there is something else to consider."

"Is this going to be one of those counsels you keep."

"It is. March, she may have thought you were one of those who were after her. Consider: she has just been attacked, and has defended herself. That was a deft maneuver, dropping her 'skip on those two men waiting for her. Then you came running at her, and shouted her name. She reacted."

"She missed. If she's that good, at that range she couldn't have missed."

"I agree. She pulled it at the last instant, probably without meaning to. Something may have told her that you were no threat."

Outside, Hoya shifted her weight back to her left leg. Myrrha tagged his arm, and led him aft to the hatchway, saying, "Let's go find out who she is."

"In retrospect, I should have told you more," said Hoya, her tone properly contrite. Although she was addressing March, her eyes kept darting furtively at Myrrha, as if she were still in amazement at the change of color motif. "Perhaps even everything," she added.

They were sitting on the bridge in sunlight filtered through the tinted Videx. March had set up mugs for them—tea for Hoya, coffee for himself and Myrrha. He thought he was drinking a lot of coffee lately. For a few moments he gazed into his mug as if to read portents in the grounds, but there were no grounds, and only his vague reflection for a portent.

"We're listening," he said, without looking up.

"Before you continue," said Myrrha. Without explanation, she tokked her Palmetto for the investment ceremony, and let Hoya watch it. Hoya's face grew increasingly perturbed as she studied the sequence.

When it was over, she said, her voice hard, "That's not me."

"We know," said Myrrha. "But who is it?"

"It looks like me," Hoya conceded. "But it's not. I was never invested."

"We know," Myrrha said again, gently this time. "We believe you."

Hoya slumped in the port captain's chair, despondent. From time to time she shook her head in disbelief. March thought that of all the events that could have occurred, this was the most unexpected.

"They just stood there and watched," Hoya whispered.

"This is why your attempts failed to contact your parents," March put in.

"Yes, I see that. They think I'm already there. As far as they know, I'm just someone shilling phony houses on a tropical planet or spaceskip warranty renewals." She then hissed a very unprincess-like string of short words.

"We're still back to who," pressed Myrrha. "Also why."

"I think," Hoya said slowly, "she might be Janesha. My mother...had a momentary weakness, a little more than a year before I was born. The girl was given to the Isaorans to raise, probably among the staff. She might well resemble me, except for the..." Suddenly she gasped. "Her nose was deliberately broken. But...but that means..."

"You've been under surveillance," said Myrrha. "We don't know for how long. Best guess is that when you moved out to Margent for university, they either stopped, or lost track of you. Hoya...what about your diary? Did you find it?"

She nodded. "And I read it from when I started at age five to my last year at Margent. There's nothing worth tearing down cottages for. Some immaturities, and floral pages, and...and a couple of boys, and some...career notes. No, it's not the diary."

"Yes, it is," said March. "It's not a specific entry or entries. It's the diary itself. It details your life from childhood to adulthood. If it can be authenticated, it proves you are the legitimate heir to the throne."

Hoya sat back, stunned. "I never thought of that."

March was scowling. "But I don't understand the succession. This Janesha can have no legitimate claim to the throne, unless..."

"Unless I am dead," said Hoya. A note of raw anger coarsened her voice. "That brings me to the last bit. I was supposed to have died on Calla Cried. Goodling knows I did not. I've learned since that he has hired an assassin named Marzanna to locate me and kill me."

"The Slavic goddess of winter and death," whispered Myrrha.

"But that suggests Goodling is ready to move," said March. "You dead, then he has the duke killed and this Janesha installed." His eyebrows merged. "But what then? What does that get him?"

"There's a little more," Hoya said quietly. She seemed hesitant to continue, but squared her shoulders and faced March directly. "There's irony in his hiring of Marzanna, because...because I am Marzanna."

# 017: Back Story

The requested information reached Alexor in the late afternoon, at refreshments. His face went slack when Cajtab whispered the answer into his ear. Slack, because he dared not show his agitation and excitement with his father in the room. With a supreme effort at self-control, he asked to be excused before the torts arrived.

Moments later in his room, Alexor slammed his right fist into his pillow, knocking it all the way to the curtains. Incoherent excitement followed in words. He was going to do this and that, and make them pay, now that he knew where they might well be.

*The Parsley Sprig.* Tavern in Carrikdove. In an airfoil he could just make it there before dark.

The anticipation of revenge tasted sweet. It eased the sting of the cut on his arm. It softened the ache of his shattered hand. He stuffed a hunting knife into a sheath at his hip, and dangled a club from his belt. Cuts for a cut, blows for a blow. He'd figure out something for Hallia when he got there.

His snarl of, "I'm coming for you!" cast a faint echo through his room.

\* \* \*

The open curtains allowed midday sunlight to flood the drawing room. In a stuffed chair positioned where the light struck, Duke Justinio warmed himself. The brief excursion with Catalina had not gone badly, but it was now clear to him that over time and neglect various differences had grown between them, and separated them. The dukedom had to be maintained, but she seemed not to consider that paramount. Instead, she was focused on exteriors: the land, the fauna and flora, the topography. He was not certain that the two interests were compatible. He himself had left environmental considerations to others, with acceptable success.

The main door opened, and into the room swept Duchess Olena. She was now attired in a floral cotton top of tight weave and a pair of black silk trousers loose enough to conceal the minor weight gain in her thighs. Now and then as she approached him, barefoot, she paused to wriggle her toes in the plush blue carpeting. Passing him by, she came to a halt at the window, blocking half the sunlight, and turned around to face him. Now the sunlight gave her a golden aura.

"It went well, I think," he said, anticipating her question. "Catalina has a wide variety of interests."

She clasped her hands together in front. "Does this trouble you, my liege?"

"She suggested that I was in thrall to my duties," he told her. "She implied that I was missing something."

"Perhaps you are. Over the centuries, perhaps we have grown stolid, even stoic. We sit in our castles and look out the windows at our domains. At least Portico the Bastard had his oil paintings."

"Is that a rebuke, my dear?"

"No, my liege." She drifted forward to lean a thigh against a chair arm, her closeness warming him. "But a little excitement, a little novelty now and then...what can it hurt? If Catalina wishes to interest herself in matters outside the castle, perhaps that is a good thing."

He gazed up at her. His voice became bland. "By implication, you are suggesting that I, we, might direct our interests there as well."

"What can it hurt?"

"So I should take you on an airfoil excursion?"

"I would love to go with you in an airfoil, my liege."

"Where would we go?"

"Anywhere." She dropped herself onto his lap and threw her arms around his neck. "Anywhere, my liege. Let the grass grow so high on the croquet field that we cannot see the wickets."

He flashed a crooked smile. "Desshelle may not approve. She works hard to keep it trimmed."

"Invite her to dinner."

His brow knotted. "Eat with the staff?"

"Why not? This segregation is not etched in stone. We declare what our lifeways are, my liege, do we not?" Her fingers ruffled his dark hair. "The majordomo has promised a trake feast tomorrow night. That would be a perfect time."

"So it would," he agreed. "I'd better have Goodling inform the kitchen staff."

She touched her lips to his forehead. "Perhaps...in a little while."

\* \* \*

The revelation from Hoya left March more puzzled than stunned. He knew she was dangerous—the incidents in front of the café and with her 'skip more than confirmed this estimate. But a hired assassin? In retrospect, certainly, she was capable. But she was also the heir to the Palologa throne—a considerably more sedate life. A glance from him at Myrrha told her to give him a moment, and she refilled their mugs.

It was Hoya who broke the uneasy silence. "You're wondering how," she said. "I understand that. I've never told anyone, except my diary. It's...private. But I think I have to tell you, so you know."

"We want to help you," March said gently. "Just tell us."

Hoya swallowed half her tea, and set her mug down in the depression on the console. Hands folded and clasped between her knees, she took a few deep breaths.

"My second year at Margent," she began. "There were rumors that a couple students, young women, had dropped out of classes without telling anyone. I supposed that this sort of thing happened, and paid scant attention to it. Then a couple more, and a couple more, over that first semester. I had a roommate at the time, Mathanella

Tabbot. Mathy, we called her. That was her field as well, math. Quiet. And shy, or maybe reserved, because she was very good in her field, almost to the point of embarrassment. As she kept trying to explain herself, everyone does something well; she just happens to do math.

"Sorry. Too much data, I guess. What happened was, she was seeing a young man named Volcolo, and... she hinted that it might be nice that evening if I studied in the library for a while, instead of in the room. I got all the way to the library before I realized I'd left my Palmetto in the room."

Here Hoya paused, and swallowed hard. A gulp of tea helped lubricate her voice again.

"There were three young men in the room when I returned. Mathy was on the bed, clothed but unconscious. The men were in the process of slipping her into a large cloth bag with a sturdy drawstring. The intent was to carry her off. I found out later that they were selling young women to traffickers."

"It is a lucrative business," Myrrha said, with quiet disgust.

"But that was later," Hoya continued. "They had drugged Mathy—something in her drink, in the wine—but I was on to them, so obviously I would not drink anything they had treated. It wasn't even a good wine. A bottle from the bottom shelf. But I...I have a black belt in aikido. I started when I was ten, with a white belt and a *gi* that weighed more than I did, and I stayed with it, and later a *sensei* at Margent put me through training for the belt. They came at me. When it was over, two were dead, and the third was out for a day or so. He was interrogated—not very gently, I understand—and that's how we found out what was going on."

"But to become an assassin," cued March.

Hoya nodded. "I'd killed two men, and left a third unable to walk again. It was thought that I was affected by the trauma of killing, but that was not the case, not at all. I was glad I had killed them. They had ruined too many lives—the loved ones and relatives of those they had drugged and sold, you see. They had earned a one-way trip through the airlock. Yes, I made that judgment. Mathy was, *is*, my friend.

"So I was recommended for counseling, and I went. I was subjected to testing and evaluation. One of the evaluators was a member of the guild, the Assassins Guild. It was determined that I had the right mindset, the right attitude, but they were wrong in that regard. I *don't* like killing. But in some instances it has to be done, for there is no other way to stop some people. So I signed on, with the strict condition that my contracts consisted of evildoers. I had a rationale: the laws, in the spiral arm and local, are poorly administered. Maybe a third of those who hurt others are detained. The others get away, they go free. The Guild has excellent investigators, better than the constabularies. But the Guild is not proactive; it doesn't take action on its own, nor does it enforce laws. Someone outside the Guild has to offer a contract. That in fact happens less often than you hear. And often the contract is meant to create a job opening for someone to advance to. Another might be against a quarrelsome neighbor. I won't touch those, ever. There are things the Guild does that are wrong in my view. Obviously there's more to it, but that's the essence. As for me, I've taken seven contracts, all against evildoers: three traffickers, two purveyors of narcotics to children, one serial rapist, and one venefice. I will never accept any other kind of contract."

"One...what?" asked March.

"Venefice. A poisoner. And that's what brings me to Goodling. The venefice and one of the traffickers had operated briefly on Faedra. I did not know it at the time, but in some way they had opposed Goodling. I only found out yesterday he was my client for those two contracts when he requested the contract to kill me. He does not know who I am, of course. In the Guild, we're all anonymous. But I'm happy to say he's going to be disappointed."

"I wonder who was poisoned," mused Myrrha.

Hoya shrugged. "I would think it were someone in one of the Families, but I'm sure I've no idea..."

Her voice trailed off, and her eyes shone with sudden deep thought. Finally she shook her head. "No," she said. "No, he wouldn't do that."

March stared hard at her. "What? Do what?"

A look of shocked disbelief came over Hoya. Horror gave her gray eyes a glow that flared for a moment, then faded as she slowly came to accept the inevitable facts. Her voice trembled as she spoke.

"I was the third child born to my parents," she said, almost inaudibly. "The first two, Mikelo and Theod, both boys, died in infancy. I don't know how soon after they were born. I don't think it was very long after. Nor do I know the cause of death, except that they simply stopped breathing. I was born two years later." Now she focused on March and Myrrha. "But what if they were killed... murdered? It's possible, and I'm afraid it's more than possible. But what could Goodling hope to gain by it?"

"The answer to that," said Myrrha, "is the same as what he gains by replacing you with Janesha. I don't think she realizes it, but she is Goodling's tool. He trained her. She'll do what he wants."

Hoya slowly nodded. "He'll be the power behind the throne."

"I don't think that's his end game," said March. "At some point he'll kill her, and if there is no issue from her marriage—if she marries at all—he'll take over. Ultimately, that's what the drive for power is all about: grab all you can get. There won't be anyone to challenge for the throne except you, and he thinks you're as good as dead."

Hoya was aghast. "But that means my father has to die first."

"It will be something subtle," said March. "Something discreet. And certainly something the majordomo will have someone else do, then kill them before they can talk to anyone." He frowned. "Is there someone in the castle who can bring us up to date?"

"I-I don't know. Maybe one of the kitchen staff. I don't know." She stood up. "But we have to go to Faedra."

"Not in your 'skip," March said. "They'll be looking for it. We'll take the *Bluebolt*. Send yours there, too, but leave it in Track, subject to remote recall. Myrrha—"

"I know, I know. Set course for Faedra and enTrack. And it's done. Three hours and two minutes, if the weather is good."

For a moment Hoya gaped at her. Then she laughed.

# 018: Best Laid Plans

The workday at *The Parsley Sprig* commenced an hour after sunrise, and with the trio of Kamie, Jinzy, and Hallia now assisting Garla the tavernkeep, setup was completed almost an hour earlier than if done by only one person. Jinzy's face was much improved, and she gave no sign that her ribs were bothering her. After a short break, during which they all had glasses of fruit juice and rolls with butter, Garla attended the kitchen while the others readied themselves for custom. A few patrons began to drift in for a light meal, and toward midday for a break from work. The atmosphere was relaxed and friendly—a setting that still left Jinzy and Hallia somewhat uneasy, being unaccustomed to it. Little encouragements from Kamie soothed them.

As they began preparations for the evening meal and the drinking, Caber and two of his colleagues, one of whom was burly and rough-looking enough to concern Kamie, entered the tavern, took up a table, and signaled to Jinzy for service. With some trepidation she approached, uncertain what to expect. It was clear that the men had just finished work for the day. She stitched a faint and perfunctory smile in place and asked if they were ready to order.

"Ales all around, please," said Caber. His ready smile both relaxed her and put her on alert. "Fish meals for us, and I'll have a small salad as well." The other two men laughed, and he added indignantly, "I like salads."

As Jinzy walked away, she overheard one of the men say, "So she's the one you were telling us about." That only heightened her tension, as she wondered what Caber had told them. While Hallia drew the ales, Jinzy moved to the ready window for the food. Beside her, Kamie told her to relax.

"I can't," she whispered. "He talked about me. I don't know what he told them, I-I..."

Kamie laid a hand on her shoulder. "Be yourself. Anyway, I don't hear them laughing, and there are no furtive glances your way as if they are talking about you."

"Meals up," Garla announced.

Jinzy placed them neatly on a tray, while Hallia ported the ale mugs. The men thanked both of them, but as Jinzy started to turn away, Caber said, "I'm glad you're working today. I was wondering whether you would be here."

She knew her face had flushed; she wanted to hide, but there was no place to turn to. Following Kamie's advice, she said bravely, "And I was wondering whether you would show up." She was on the verge of more words when fisherfolk and shopkeepers wandered in, and for the next half hour she was busier than she had ever been in the castle.

"He seems nice," Kamie told her at one point. Jinzy had no idea how to respond to that. "Just relax, Jinzy."

"I'm *trying*," she hissed. Hallia handed her three filled mugs for Caber's table. A deep breath failed to stabilize her, but she forced herself calm as she approached the table. One by one she placed the mugs.

After she straightened, the tavern door opened, and in walked Alexor.

\* \* \*

After the midday meal, for the third day in a row Catalina boarded the airfoil prepped for her and took off for unplanned points. The more she traveled, the more she enjoyed it. So much around her was new and unfamiliar and therefore of major curiosity. This time she followed the meandering Fiumal river for three hours, all the way to the Golubic Ocean, where she docked on the empty beach west of the river and simply basked in the sights. A few meditative breaths cleared her mind as she sat on the sand, so that she was able to absorb the view without focusing on any particular part of it. Now and then her idle fingers combed through the fine yellow sand, taking in the texture and sunlit warmth of it. Twice she nodded off, and caught herself.

Presently she rose, and began walking without aim. The waves seemed to call to her in some primordial language, as if to say, "Look at us." Not to persuade her to dive in, but merely to become aware of the reality of them. Sometimes she was close enough to the ocean that the foam from the breakers hissed and died at her boots. The dry sand yielded under her weight, making her stagger. A breeze came up, laden with salt and brine, and tousled her hair. Most of all, no one scolded her or reminded her of her place in the family.

From a cargo pocket of her trousers Catalina removed a flat silver tin, opened the lid, and removed a fruit-scented cheroot and an igniter. Never before had she smoked, or even considered it. A few members of the household staff used tobacco, and she wondered what the attraction was. Discreetly she had studied how they went about it. Now she stuck one end between her lips, fired the other end, and drew smoke into her mouth and lungs. And coughed, spitting out the cheroot in the process. Experimentation soon enabled her to inhale without reaction. She did not particularly enjoy smoking, but it was a different activity, and best of all, it was undoubtedly frowned upon by Snarrel Goodling. But she tucked the tin and igniter back into her pocket, and only smoked half the cheroot before extinguishing it in the sand and burying it there.

To the west, the orange dwarf that held Faedra in thrall was halfway to the horizon. Perhaps four hours of daylight remained. She might head back to the castle now, or travel west along the coast to a fishing village called Carrikdove. She might stay overnight in the castle, or assert herself by staying overnight somewhere in the village.

For another hour she wandered over the beach, taking it all in while she considered what to do. In the end, she decided she was not quite ready to behave so radically as to stay out overnight.

\* \* \*

Jinzy scarcely had time to back away. In that moment, never had she felt more alone and defenseless. Her racing heart drummed. The look on Alexor's face approached madness as he drew the knife from his belt and stalked toward her.

"Don't know where she is?" he shouted. *"You don't know where she is?* You're nothing but a *lying kitchen quiff.* I'll teach you—"

In that moment Kamie stepped between them and tried to grab his knife hand. In the process, she turned the blade toward herself. The razor-sharp point swept across her ribs before she twisted the weapon away from him and cast it aside. It clattered across the floor, where a patron scooped it up and set it carefully on the table. Kamie winced as pain and shock began to seep in, and she clutched at herself as she spilled onto a bench.

From somewhere within Jinzy arose a thunderstorm of anger. She stepped forward and slugged Alexor across the left eye and cheek with her fist. The unexpected blow stunned him, and before he could collect himself to respond to it, a few men began to gather behind him, intent on intervention. Caber reached him first, and spun him around. A fist hardened by hard work slammed into Alexor's nose and brought an eruption of blood as he staggered back a step.

Rage as if from a volcano spewed from Alexor, but shocked sudden pain turned his shout into a shriek. "Do you know who I am!"

The answer was the sound of a beaten gong, the kind from a temple that resounds throughout the mountains and calls the faithful to prayer. Alexor pitched forward, eyes scrolled up, so unconscious that when he fell, he did not break that fall with his hands and arms. He landed face-down and audibly on the gritty hardwood floor. Standing over him was Garla, ruefully examining the now-warped aluminum skillet in her right hand. Despite her relatively small stature, her demeanor was that of a mother bear defending her cubs.

Jinzy had two reactions. The first was to say, "I think he's...maybe he's dead."

"Don't tease me," Kamie said roughly, a little trickle of blood leaking between her fingers.

In the next moment, a tear in each eye, Jinzy was standing before Caber. She seemed not to know what to do next. Tenderly he held out his arms to her, and she collapsed against him. "Thank you," she whispered into the side of his neck.

"Any time."

"He's still alive," said Garla. "Help me cast him out onto the glideway. Hallia, summon the physician," she added, with a look to Kamie, and gave her the Palmetto code.

"If I may?" said Caber's burly companion, stepping forward. "Scoober Paddy has a trawler leaving tomorrow morning to fish for snorks. They run in schools in the deep waters about five hundred clicks out. The trawler will be gone for half a year," here he glanced up at the ceiling, as if trying to recall some fact, "and I think their next port of call is Voglebay."

"Snorks?" said Kamie, still seated on the bench. She seemed to be recovering a little from the initial shock of the cut, and her voice was strong. "The ones with all the teeth?"

The big man nodded. "They say it takes three bites before you learn how to handle them properly out of the nets." He nudged Alexor with the toe of his boot. "Some folks even longer."

"That's...Voglebay, isn't that on the other side of Faedra," said Hallia. To Garla she gave a nod and said, "Doctor Lawal is on his way.

The big man turned to Jinzy, who had just pulled away from Caber, her face flushed. "It's a hard piece of work on the boats, *dobra*," he told her, "and if one does not pull his weight or behave himself, one might 'accidentally' fall overboard, probably at night when everyone else is too asleep or drunk to hear the cries for help. One way or another, *dobra*, I don't think you will ever see this," and now he kicked Alexor, "chunk of chum again."

"If you would, please, Tomo," said Garla.

Tomo threw Alexor over his shoulder like a sack of grain. As Caber moved to assist, Tomo blocked him with a thick arm and said, "No, Halvor and I have this. You stay here and see to your friend. We'll see you in the morning on the docks. Don't stay up too late." With a parting nod and a, "*Dobra*," to Jinzy, he and Halvor departed.

Still lamenting her skillet, Garla turned to address the patrons in the bay. "Nothing to worry about," she said to them. "Just taking out some trash. Hallia, let's start drawing ales for these thirsty folks. Kamie, you stay right there and wait for Doctor Lawal."

\* \* \*

"It's going to be night by the time we arrive at Faedra," said March.

He and the two women were standing before the empty Videx on the bridge of the *Bluebolt*, having grown tired of sitting down in the captain's chairs and on the murphy bench. As yet, only the planet was the destination; they had yet to select a specific site on its surface. Faedra Spaceport was on the other side of the planet from Wanderby, but Myrrha told them there were several adjunct docksites that served various towns and villages.

"Suggestions?" March asked tersely, now leaning back against the console. He looked and felt tired, and this was present in his tone. In the past few days, sleep had come rarely, and of short duration. Also frustrating was the fact that he still had no idea what they were to accomplish, only that there was urgency to the accomplishment. Far easier it was to hijack a shipment of ingots—but he had abandoned that part of his life.

"I want to try to reach someone in Palologa Castle," answered Hoya. "Whoever I can reach, to learn the talk of what's going on there. Otherwise, we'll be bounding into a situation we don't understand."

Myrrha nodded agreement. "There are several villages along the coast," she told March. But only a couple of them have shops that let airfoils. We can't very well downdock within sight of the castle, because that would alert someone that help—"

"Snarrel Goodling," Hoya put in.

"...is on the way. Yes, Goodling. But he'll have help, and we don't know who it will be. So we lark about in one of the villages tonight, Hoya reaches someone, and we plan from there. We're looking for a place with decent ale and some comestibles. The two villages we should consider are equidistant from the castle."

"Pick one," said March, more than ready to go aft to the stateroom and lie down.

"Already done," said Myrrha. "Black Rock."

"I know of no such place," wondered Hoya.

"The Irish would say Carrikdove."

# 019: Long and Winding Road

Over a quarter of an hour, Doctor Lawal—a tall and rangy black man in his fifties—managed to clean and disinfect the ten-centimeter cut along Kamie's left side, just above the floating ribs; stitch the cut together and secure it with little bridge bandages that clung to the skin like barnacles; take the mandatory tiny sample of her blood to check her identity against the DNA database; and caution her to avoid strenuous activity for the next three days, at which point he would return to remove the bridges and check the healing.

Meanwhile, Jinzy had brought her a fresh top, this one red. "So if you start bleeding again, the patrons won't notice," she explained the color, a wry grin quirking her face. Kamie responded with a wan smile.

Gradually the evening crowd thinned, and Kamie pulled light duty. Lawal sat at a table by himself; every minute or so he glanced at his Palmetto, obviously awaiting a message. A couple of solitaries entered the tavern, intent on one last ale before heading home. Initial cleanup began, with Garla attending the stove.

Lawal's frown deepened with the passing of the minutes. He turned his ale mug this way and that, and peered into it the way a seer analyzed entrails. Whatever answers he received were profoundly unsatisfactory.

Kamie favored her left side as she helped restore the tables to their original disposition in the bay. Aware of this activity, Lawal scowled at her until she abandoned her efforts and sat down on a bench. Dismay on her face said that she hated to watch others working while she sat and did nothing. Her hands fidgeted in frustration.

Moments later, Lawal stared hard at his Palmetto. It was clear that he had received the information he sought, and that it was far and away not what he had expected. After a brief lapse into pensiveness, he motioned for Kamie to join him at the table.

Forearm and elbow pressed against her left ribs, Kamie sat down across the table from him. Briefly he hesitated, as if he were uncertain regarding the approach to what he had to tell her. This worried Kamie, and showed in her face. She lofted both eyebrows at him.

"You said you worked in the kitchen in Isaora Castle," Lawal began slowly, though his speech was clipped. "Basic kitchen help. How long have you done this, if I might ask?"

"I started when I was...I don't know, maybe five," she replied. "So that would be twenty-three years. But I had other duties as well. For example, I filled in for one of the assistant groundskeepers on occasion." Her face twisted. "Why? What's wrong?"

"What?" He seemed remote, searching for a way through a delicate situation. "Oh, nothing is...wrong, if that is the correct word here. But there is nothing in your blood to suggest a heritage in the Isaoran household."

Kamie flashed a grin. "That's probably why I was limited to kitchen and other duties," she said, adding cheerfully, "I'm just a simple peasant girl."

"That's not what I..." He heaved a long sigh. "I'm not sure I can explain this properly. You may have done scullery work, but that is not who you are. According to DNA analysis, you are Palologan."

Kamie's eyes narrowed. "I-I don't understand."

"Specifically, you are a daughter of Justinio Palologa."

She gasped. "I'm...*what*?"

"In fact, you are his eldest daughter. But not..." He swallowed a lump. "Not by the duchess."

"There must be some mistake," she countered, shaking her head violently. "I'm Kamie Isaora. As far back as I can remember, I've been Kamie Isaora."

"Adopted by the Isaorans, perhaps," said Lawal. "Or given to them by Palologa to raise, out of sight and out of mind. This happens with...outlier births; not often at all, but it does happen."

"No. No, no, you're wrong. This has to be wrong."

He leaned a little closer, and spoke very softly, his dark face somber. "There is no mistake in DNA, Kamie... Lady Palologa. Please believe me."

"I-I..." She called out to Garla. "May I please have an ale?" After the acknowledgement, Kamie asked him, "Do you know who my mother is?"

Lawal's lips paled as they tightened. "I do. But..."

"Oh, you have to tell me!" she cried.

For a long moment he looked away, at the walls and the windows and anywhere but at Kamie. At last he gave himself a little nod, as if he had made up his mind regarding a particularly difficult question.

"Your mother," he said, now looking directly at her so that there could be no mistaking his words, "is about to bring you a mug of ale."

\* \* \*

Somewhere during the journey back to the castle, Catalina changed her mind. She still had more than enough time to reach it before dark, but something within her needed more than that. She wanted to dare herself, to take a chance. To take a risk. A taut communication with her mother explained what she intended to do. Rather to her surprise, the duchess acquiesced, along with a caution to be careful.

The permission dulled the effect of the daring. She almost changed her mind again. What was the point if she was allowed to do something that should have been frowned upon? That she should have been discouraged from doing. She almost hoped something would happen to her. But she pressed on toward the west coast. Carrikdove was but two hours away. Or three, if she slowed after darkness fell.

\* \* \*

The kitchen maid's name was Cinya, and she was medium in many ways: height, brownness of hair and eyes, pale complexion, garb. In short, she might have been anonymous and invisible in a crowd. In Goodling's room, she was cowed but attentive as she stood not three paces from where he was sitting in a stuffed chair, hands modestly clasped in front of her. He decided against using her now. He wanted no distractions from what she had to do, and he certainly did not want her in discomfort tomorrow evening.

"Unless Hallia returns, food service would fall to me, sire," she said, her tone low and deferential. She would not quite look at him. "I assure you that I will perform my best duty when I serve the duke."

"Of course you will," soothed Goodling. In no wise did he wish to alert her. "Of course. But with Hallia away, it is incumbent upon me to be certain that everything proceeds just so. You understand that?"

"Of course, sire. I shall do my utmost."

"I've no doubt of that, Cinya. So tell me, how do you mean to serve the meal to the duke?"

She replied brokenly, as if she were not prepared for the question. "I, well, I receive the plate of trake from the cook and carefully place it before the duke. You know, I have done this before..." She looked away, hoping not to have given offense.

Her reticence left Goodling pleased with himself. Tomorrow night, when it was all over, he meant to celebrate with Cinya extensively before he eliminated her as a witness.

"And what else?" he asked her.

"A small bowl of boiled vegetables—"

"Which he probably will refuse to eat," Goodling put in.

Cinya had to laugh. "Yes, sire, I know. But..."

"But it has to be done, yes." Appearances and procedures must be preserved. "Go on, please."

"And let me see...there's a silver bell creamer in the cooler with that clear sauce for baked fish that he likes," she went on. "I'll pour that over the fish before I bring it to him. Oh, and he will want water during the meal and an ale afterwards." She glanced hopefully in his direction. "I think that's all, sire."

"Indeed it is," he told her. "Now, I want you to focus your attention on the duke. Trake is his favorite fish. Renetta will serve the duchess, so you need not concern yourself with her."

"Yes, sire." She hesitated. "I have a question."

A mild alarm shot through the majordomo. Any deviation might well become conspicuous following the events of the dinner. "Ask it."

"Do I stand by the duke while he eats, or should I wait in the kitchen to be summoned?"

"Custom dictates that you stand to the duke's left, and three or four steps behind him," Goodling told her.

"I just wanted to be sure, sire."

"Of course. Until tomorrow evening, then."

After a curtsey, she left the room.

\* \* \*

The Duchess Palologa awoke because her bed was cold. Soon enough, she learned the reason: she was alone in it. Justinio's name was almost on her lips when she spotted him standing in front of the great floor-to-ceiling window. Hands clasped behind his back, he was gazing out into the night. For a while she watched him; at no point did he even move. A bit of worry crept into her, and she got up to go to him, her pastel green silk nightgown swirling softly around her legs. The sound seemed to stir him, and he glanced in her direction.

"I did not mean to awaken you," he said.

"It was the solitude that awoke me, my liege." She moved to stand close beside him, and peered through the window.

"What do you see?" he asked her.

"I see darkness. It is, after all, night."

Justinio did not respond to this, nor did he even glance at her.

"What do you see, my liege?" she asked.

For a long moment he did not answer her. When at last he did speak, his words seemed to come from far away.

"I was but a boy of eight or nine," he said, remembering. "Training had not yet begun. I stayed out...one night I stayed out late, worrying my parents. I had gone out a ways from the castle, to a point where there was just enough light for me not to run into things. But where did the light come from? I was curious. Finally I found it, in the sky. Countless points of light, all adding themselves together."

"The stars," said Olena.

"Yes. The stars. It was not the first time I had seen them, but it was the first that I had noticed them." He reached out to adjust a curtain away from the window jamb. "A memory, yes, but lost in time, until..."

"My liege?"

"The trip with Catalina did not go as well as planned, for her or for myself," he went on. "I told you it went well. I suppose it did, but...Olena, she sees things that I used to see, and long ago stopped seeing. Rivers, trees, creatures, sounds, smells, the feel of grass..."

Gently the duchess leaned against him.

"I feel I've lost something," he said. "And I don't know what it is. But I want to find it."

"Yes."

He turned to her. "Do you feel it as well?"

"We have limited ourselves to our ways, my lie... Justinio." She laid a hand on his arm. "It is not a loss that you feel, but a limitation, one that you, we, have imposed upon ourselves because that is our way. It has been the way of the duchies for centuries now. All our doors are unlocked, but we never go through them."

"Except to visit another duchy," he pointed out.

"Yes. Except that. And that, not very often."

Justinio unclasped his hands and placed them on the windowsill, arms locked as he leaned forward. "I'm tired...no, not that. I feel weary in some way."

A note of sympathy touched her tone. "I believe I would like to go on a walk with you tomorrow," she said.

He nodded agreement. "Where shall we go?"

"It does not matter, my liege."

He smiled. "Catalina would have said that."

"She would simply have gone?"

"She would have, indeed. She said as much to me on our...excursion. I'm beginning to wonder..." His voice trailed off. He turned to face her. "Wonder whether she truly wishes to be Duchess. I believe she wants something more."

"She does not need to be crowned just yet, my liege."

He glanced past her at the bed. "I believe I could sleep now."

She led him back to the bed.

\* \* \*

The reunion in *The Parsley Sprig* was tearful. Once the evidence had been presented and the relationship established, Garla broke down, and Kamie with her. Caber, the last of the patrons, having an early fishing trip scheduled, departed for the night after a quiet moment with Jinzy, followed shortly thereafter by Doctor Lawal. Jinzy and Hallia finished closing down, and went upstairs to their room.

Garla and Kamie, straddling a bench to face one another, found themselves alternating between both talking at once and saying nothing at all. Kamie did not know her own mind at the moment. A grown woman who had assumed she was an orphan or abandoned, she had long outgrown the need to know her lineage. Garla, on the other hand, having—as she had explained through tears—been compelled to surrender her infant daughter to the care and disposition of the Palologas, had eventually secured the memory in a locked box in her mind, never to be opened again or even noticed.

"I didn't know," Garla began saying, over and over again.

Finally a touch from Kamie quelled the repetition. She peered into her empty mug, then slid it to the center of the table. "Two of those is enough," she said. "At the castle we don't get much wine or ale to drink."

"But you were treated well?" Garla pressed once more, seeking to assuage her sense of guilt.

Kamie made a face. "As well as could be expected, I suppose. Scullery is long hours, and it's also work that has to please people who can criticize you merely because they have that power and position. I don't think they realize what they're doing...well, most of them don't. There are a few exceptions."

"Like that young man who's going on a prolonged fishing trip."

"Him, yes. But Garla...hmm. I suppose I should call you Amma now. Garla, my ancestry is what it is. It's been written. This is now. I am writing this moment, and must prepare to write the next day. What's changed is that I get to write it with my Amma, my mother."

Garla began to weep again. "I didn't know," she said.

Kamie reached out to touch her. "Whatever offense you think you've committed, Amma, I forgive you. I'm glad you're in my life again."

The tears became a flood, but Kamie handed her a napkin. "It's written, Amma. Please don't cry. I'm here."

Garla sniffled, and nodded, and soon passed back to Kamie a very soggy napkin. She took it upstairs with her.

An hour later, with the stove cleaned and the tables more or less rearranged to their original positions, Garla took stock, surveying with approval the overall layout. She hoped the next day would prove quieter—as the great majority of the days were. She was about to lock up when the front door opened.

A tall young woman with long hair the color of orange Solntsa on a clear day entered the tavern. Her blue eyes gazed about, and finally settled on the tavernkeep.

"We're closing up," said Garla.

"Oh. I'm so sorry." She made a little gesture at a window. "I saw the light was on, and I..."

"I understand." Kindly she asked, "What did you want?"

"Oh. Just a room for the night...if you have one free. If that's all right. And I've docked my airfoil outside, but off the glideway, if that's all right."

Garla nodded. "It's a gold a night, and do be quiet. Others are sleeping upstairs, as I soon will be. You may have Room 2. The key is in the lock. Breakfast in the morning is comp with the room."

The woman passed her a coin. "Yes, thank you, and I'll be quiet. I've had a bit of a journey today. Oh, and my name is Catalina."

"Catalina..."

She shook her head. "Just Catalina. And I'll be gone after breakfast. You probably won't see me again. And...good night to you, and thank you."

Garla watched her ascend the steps, and pocketed the coin.

# 020: The Plot Thickens

It was well dark and *The Parsley Sprig* staff was fast asleep—Kamie on her right side to protect her ribs—when a Palmetto pinged. Some stirring followed, but when the second ping sounded, Hallia rolled over and fumbled around among her things on the floor, finally to retrieve the culprit. By this time, Kamie and Jinzy were also well awake.

"Lights ten percent," ordered Kamie, and sat up, to find Hallia looking distressed. Instantly worried, she asked, "What is it?"

Hallia hesitated. "I'm not...sure. I have this on mute, so we can talk, but I-I...this is weird."

Kamie patted a spot beside her on the bed. Jinzy joined them as well. Hallia displayed her Palmetto for them to see. There was no image in the screen, only an icon that indicated a non-visual transmission.

"She claims to be Hoya Catalina Palologa," said Hallia. Her dark, gray-brown eyes were filled with confusion. As she leaned over the Palmetto, locks of pale brown hair fell over her eyes. In frustration she swept them back over her shoulder. "She has visual on her end, and it took her a moment to recognize me. But she sees me almost every day." Worry filled her tone. "Maybe they're trying to find me, to take me back."

Kamie shook her head. "They wouldn't send the princess. The majordomo would be tasked with your return, and he would send one of his people. No, whatever this is, it's something else."

"But...should I even talk with her?"

"If we're to find out what this is, I'd say we have to, Hallia. Just don't offer information until we know more."

"All right," Hallia said, and turned the mute off. "How do I know you are Hoya Catalina?" she asked.

"It's complicated," came the response. "I've been away for fourteen years."

Shocked, Hallia hit the mute again. Large wide eyes turned to Kamie. "This cannot be. But...but it sounds a little like her."

"Request visual," Jinzy suggested.

Hallia did so. The reply was immediate and certain. "I'm not sure I want to do that at this time. Not until I know what's happening. Is someone there with you? Is that why you keep muting me?"

"May I?" asked Kamie. Hallia passed her the Palmetto. "I'm Kamie Isaora," she told the voice at the other end. "Perhaps I can help."

"I remember that name, and...I know your face. You've changed a little, but that's to be expected." Now the woman sounded uneasy. "Did Hallia take up service with the Isaorans while I was away?"

Kamie laughed lightly, and blunted her answer. "It's complicated. You said you wanted to know what's happening. Could you be more specific?"

A long and hesitant silence followed. The Palmetto sent a deep breath, as if the woman were about to take a chance. "Can anyone else hear me?" she asked.

"Listening are myself, Hallia, and Jinzy Isaora. No one else."

"I think my parents are in danger," said Hoya. "I fear it will come within the next two days or so."

"You must have a reason for telling us this."

"I have already survived two assassination attempts. I now have direct knowledge that an assassin from the Guild has been contracted against me. Is that reason enough?"

"Who *are* you?" Hallia asked bravely. "I have seen the princess almost every day for the past twelve years, ever since she returned from school for her investment. So who are *you*?"

Hoya seemed to ignore this. "It will be something subtle, and the majordomo will be behind it. He will probably employ someone as an unwitting agent. I think it may well be you, Hallia."

*"Oh my goddesses..."*

More silence followed. The sound of a throat clearing came from the Palmetto, followed by, "Hallia, what are you doing in Carrikdove at this time of night?"

"Mute," ordered Kamie.

Hallia emphatically shook her head. "Whoever you are, know that Goodling uses me—or used me, I say, because he never will again. But I-I can see how he has also been...I don't know...preparing me? It's not clear. And since I work...worked in the kitchen..."

"Are you saying you've run away from Palologa Castle?" Hoya asked.

"The three of us are refugees," Kamie told her. "We will not return to our respective Families."

"It will be a poison of some kind," said Hoya. The strain in her voice said she was forcing calm upon herself. "You would not know that you are administering it."

"I wouldn't administer it at all, because I am not going back," said Hallia. "I think that would be Cinya. With me gone, she becomes the senior food server, and would start with tomorrow's dinner attending the duke and duchess."

"Tomorrow night?" said Hoya, alarm in her voice.

"It's nothing," said Hallia. "A simple dinner."

They heard a long sigh. "Right. All right. I have to think about this."

"Wait," cried Kamie. But Hoya had already closed out.

\* \* \*

Despite his efforts, Satrin Hommer was unable to tell the majordomo anything useful regarding the wayward Isaoran kitchen staff. The Isaoran ducal family and Cajtab's small staff had proved closed-mouthed to discreet inquiries. The scullery and maintenance staff were suspicious. Hommer was able to learn only the names of the two runaways. Neither registered with Goodling.

Late at night the majordomo sat in his sleeping quarters, idly sketching on a scrap of paper. Now that the coming day was almost upon him, he wanted it to be over without having to go through the motions. Much that might go awry had been stabilized by precautions. Still, runaway staff were rare; two from Isaora and Hallia from Palologa might signify something, but try as he might, Goodling was unable to discern what was once called a spanner in the works. Three missing kitchen quiffs hardly constituted a threat to his plans. Nevertheless, he bore it in mind while he sketched.

At length he glanced at the scrap of paper. There were no portents, only an incoherent meandering of black lines with no apparent beginning or end. He wondered whether that very formlessness was itself a portent. Unexpectedly, the thought made him shiver.

\*   \*   \*

Frustrated and annoyed, Hoya flounced onto the port captain's chair and tossed her Palmetto onto the instrumentation console. "They don't believe me," she groused at Myrrha, on the murphy bench.

"Would you, in their place?" she retorted. "At least we may have discovered the killing ground."

"There are always two guards present at the banquet hall, armed only with halberds," said Hoya. "They have no function save for show. But they will prevent an intrusion, unless we open fire, which I do not want to do."

"So we prevent the duke and duchess from attending the dinner," said March.

Hoya exhaled loudly. "That might prevent the deaths for the time being," she said. "But there's no evidence that Goodling is even planning anything. My claims against him would not be credible, especially as I would be the imposter." She barked a mirthless laugh. "Imposter. Do you want to know the truth? I don't want to be Duchess of Palologa. I have a career. It may be frowned upon in some quarters, but in the end I do some good. I don't want to sit around in a tower all my life." She stared down at her feet on the deck. "But I don't want my parents killed."

"We have our mission, then," Myrrha said, to March. "Protect her parents and stop Goodling."

March nodded. "But we have to do it in such a way that they are safe and Goodling is exposed." He made a face. "And we have to get into the castle to do that. We're missing something. There's another factor here, a missing piece. But what is it?"

"I need to convince Hallia of my identity," said Hoya. "There is no other way."

"We'll reach Carrikdove about three hours after sunup locally," said Myrrha. "I've already cleared downdock with their Spaceport Annex."

March began, "And we'll need to let—"

"An airfoil," Myrrha said smugly. "Already done."

For a long moment Hoya studied her. "May I ask?" At Myrrha's nod of assent, she went on. "You're a 'skipcomp. A computer..."

"I am a woman. But it's complicated, Hoya. What is it that you wish to know?"

Hoya struggled for words. "I'm not sure I know what to ask. You're impossible, yet clearly here you are."

Myrrha smiled. "You want to know how I came to exist."

"Maybe that's the right question."

She glanced at March. "It was a time about two years ago. He was lonely, and sad, and a bit lost."

Hoya frowned. "I don't understand."

"One of my directives as a 'skip's computer is to attend and maintain the morale of the crew," Myrrha explained. "For the *Bluebolt*, a crew of one. In this case, I determined that the optimal solution to alleviate his depression was a companion, so as a computer I created the person, the entity...the *woman* you see before you, to among other things lift his spirits."

"But you have spontaneous responses to stimuli," Hoya pointed out. "That is a characteristic of life itself."

Myrrha laughed. "Yes. The computer created me... or I created myself...as a living being, so that I have spontaneous responses, and am not programmed to have them. You see the difference? Programmed, I am an android. Spontaneous, I am human. I laugh because I find some things amusing; I do not analyze them first, even for a nanosecond, to determine whether they are amusing. I have the requisite nerve endings, the sensitivities, just as you do, so that when I experience an orgasm, I do not instruct myself to calculate the proper moment for such a response. I simply experience it, the entire process. Moreover, I can and have initiated coition; I have physical desires, just as you do. They are not calculated; rather, they lead to an attempt to get March into bed. Or onto a table in the galley."

Shocked, Hoya drew back. "But I...I ate off that table."

"So did March," Myrrha added cattily, and flashed a toothy grin.

Her responses staggered, Hoya was uncertain whether to laugh. "Not only are you impossible, you're exasperating."

Another grin. "I try."

A moment passed. "So in a way these desires are in fact calculated," argued Hoya, with just a hint of mockery.

A light chuckle escaped Myrrha. "In the sense that you mean, that of seduction, yes, sometimes they are."

"But his mood is much improved, I think, and yet you are still here."

"I fell in love," Myrrha said simply.

# 021: Shocks and Stratagems

In bed, Kamie tossed restlessly, with guilt hovering over her. She owed no allegiance to Palologa, but neither now to Isaora, yet something was terribly amiss within both families and, by extension, with Lascora. The lack of bonds might have been tolerable, now that she and her two companions were shot of the families; but other innocents were also at risk. Cinya, Hallia's colleague in the kitchen, was about to be used, surely unwittingly, in a crime of regicide. If this strange Hoya was involved, either the danger extended to her or she was herself the danger. And if she were indeed the rightful princess, who was the princess living in Palologa? Finally, how far did the net extend? Were she and Jinzy and Hallia still in danger? Alexor was gone, but compared to Snarrel Goodling, he was a mere nuisance.

"Can't sleep?" whispered Jinzy.

"I want to do something, but I don't know what it is," Kamie replied.

In the dark, Jinzy sat up. "Same here."

"I have this feeling that something is missing," Kamie went on. "Something else needs to happen."

"I know," said Hallia, joining the midnight chorus. "Maybe it's Cinya. Or that Hoya. Or someone or something completely unknown to us."

"Maybe it will be clearer in the morning," Jinzy told them. "We can't warn anyone. Who would believe us? And what would we tell them, anyway?"

"And if we returned, we'd be punished," Hallia threw in. "I'd rather be...be..."

"Free?" supplied Kamie.

"Such a sweet word."

Jinzy yawned and stretched. "Let's just get what rest we can," she suggested. "No matter what happens tomorrow, we're going to need it."

That motion was seconded and carried.

Morning arrived much too quickly, and left Kamie wondering whether she had slept at all, even though she was certain she had not remained awake all the time. She roused the others, and they prepared for the day. None spoke of their nocturnal conversation, for none could find new words for it.

Garla greeted them with her customary ebullience when they reached the last step. Already the tavern door was open, and briny air added to the lingering alcohol and tobacco in the bay. A few gusts of wind soon cleared out all the aromas except that of biscuits baking, which reminded the three that they had yet to eat this morning.

But breakfast perforce had to wait, for work came first. Kamie reflected that this priority was similar to that in the Isaora kitchen, except that the treatment and the pay was infinitely better. With four to do the work of one, they were set up within the hour, and were able to take a short break.

Upstairs, a door opened. "A lodger," Garla explained. Footfalls on the steps got their attention, and when the lodger came into view, Kamie shot to her feet, mouth agape. The woman stopped at the bottom of the stairs, and gaped back at her.

Words died on Kamie's lips. She stepped closer, the better to see. To be sure. Finally she spoke. "Jan... Janesha?"

The woman continued to stare, but at the sound of the name she began to sway and totter. Her eyes scrolled up white. Kamie rushed forward, and caught her before she hit the floor.

\* \* \*

Cinya prepared and served breakfasts in the Palologa Castle, all the while well aware that Snarrel Goodling was hovering in the background. She had anticipated something like this, for this was her first day as senior in the kitchen, and it fell among his duties to see that she performed hers to perfection. This did nothing to calm her nerves. From time to time, plates clattered, glassware clinked, and silverware rang, until finally she had to stand very still, draw a few long breaths, and force herself to relax. In the background, Goodling watched her do this, but made no remark on it before he wandered away, his lips neither approving nor frowning. Cinya drew one more slow breath; steady now, she resumed her duties.

\* \* \*

A whiff of weak ammonia brought Janesha/Catalina around. She sneezed, and rubbed her nose. She was sprawled on a bench, leaning back against the table. A cushion fashioned from a folded pullover had been placed between her spine and the table's edge. Eyes open, she gradually brought people into focus—faces hovering around her like moons to her planet. Two she recognized, one better than the other: Kamie Isaora, and one of the Palologa food servers. But Kamie...

*Kamie*! She cried it out loud, her voice carrying with it joy and surprise. But more than that, she remembered. She *remembered*!

Memories flooded in, overwhelming the dam erected by years of statin treatments and by years of being told who she was supposed to be. Not that she was aware of the medication, but of the deluge. The Isaora kitchen, not long after she could walk. An older girl, two years older, taking her under wing, keeping her away from sharp objects and hot ovens and from containers with no lids on them. No cuts, no burns, no spills. A slip now and then on a greasy floor. An older girl who scarcely knew more than she did, but was good enough to share what little she did know.

Loading and storing foodstuffs, together. Cutting this and chopping that, together. Graduation to cookery, a bit of baking, together. Tending a nick, soothing a bruise, comforting an ache, icing a burn. And growing, growing, always growing taller, until she and the older girl were equal in height despite the age difference. The older girl. Her best...her only friend. Kamie Isaora.

Someone handed her a dry hand-towel, and she sobbed into it. The fabric garbled what few words she was able to utter.

A memory of loss. At the age of nine she recalled being taken away to Palologa Castle. Why, why? A big man, sometimes harsh, sometimes determined, always prodding her to do this or that correctly. But why? He called her Catalina, not Janesha. He told her she used to be called Hoya, but she was a big girl now, and old enough to be called Catalina, a name she herself had chosen...

"No, I didn't," she murmured into the towel. "It was chosen for me by you."

Investment. Rules. Procedures. Hold your head up, you're a princess. A smack across the back of the head for emphasis, or for reminder. Something wrong with her nose that had to be fixed. Appa, who was Appa? And Amma? These are your parents. Now she saw that she should have questioned this. Questioned everything. But it was all so fuzzy. The big man said...he said...he was always saying this and that, and she had to remember, remember...

Seated on the bench, Janesha screamed. And what she screamed was, "I am Janesha!"

"Yes," Kamie said softly, seated close by, her arm around Janesha's shoulder. "Yes, you are."

They turned to face one another.

"I saw you," said Janesha. "Several times, I think. From a window, or a balcony. You would wave to me. I remember...remember wondering who you were. I knew you were someone, someone..."

"And I wondered why you didn't know me," said Kamie.

"I *did* know you. But I didn't, too." She began to cry again. "I knew my name. In the kitchen, where we met, I knew my name. I remember...he was in place of my father. He said he was sent by my mother. He said I had to live here. Here with you. With you in the kitchen. That I could not live with her. I didn't know why. I don't know why. But then I was taken away, taken to Palologa...back to Palologa. I was told...oh, goddesses, I was told I was a princess, and that he was still my father, and this man said...he was saying..." She clapped her hands to her head and wailed, "It's all so clear, but so fuzzy..."

"It's all right, Janesha," Kamie whispered. "I'm here. I'm right here."

Janesha drew a breath, and another, not quite gasping. "Two days ago I rode with him in an airfoil. I remember being taught to pilot one. We went out to the plains and the river. And we talked. I told him...what I saw, what I wanted. I don't think he understood." She dropped the towel on the floor. "He is my father. Kamie... is he really my father?"

"I don't know," said Kamie, and glanced at Garla. "Doctor Lawal?" she asked.

"His airfoil just docked outside."

"Why?" asked Janesha, suddenly alarmed. "What's going on?"

"That's what we're trying to find out," said Kamie.

Janesha accepted this. To Garla, she said, "May I please have a cup of coffee?"

With Janesha, Lawal was as tender as he had been with Kamie the evening before. After treating her with a mild sedative for emotional shock, he drew a thin tube of blood from her and let the Palmetto analyze it for drugs, disease, and identity. In the meantime, she drained two mugs of coffee, often sighing between sips. All the while, Kamie Isaora sat next to her, and even held her hand on the bandage over the small vein from which Lawal had drawn blood.

Waiting for the results, Lawal asked Kamie, "How are your ribs this morning?"

"Achy," she replied. "I'll live. Truth is, I'd forgotten about them until you reminded me."

Lawal had the grace to look sheepish, and quickly changed the subject. "I'm sure there is much more to the story than what little you have told me so far," he said. "I place no faith in rumors, but as three of you are refugees from Wanderby, I might surmise that matters lately are not going well there. As two of you are my patients for now, if there is something you think I can do or tell you, please do ask."

"Thank you," said Kamie. "But right now I wouldn't even know what to ask."

"Tell him," urged Hallia.

Kamie made a face at her. "We think there may be a plot against Palologa," she said, deliberately vague. "We have no proof, and know of no participants. We might make guesses, but..."

Lawal nodded. "The dukes have been around for three centuries now," he said, thinking aloud. "They have grown stale, and set in their ways. I suppose someone of the right...or perhaps I should say wrong, disposition might regard that staleness as weakness."

He might have said more, but his Palmetto pinged, announcing the results of the analyses of Janesha's blood. As he had frowned the night before, so did he now as well. But on this occasion, he did not hesitate to speak.

"Janesha, this is personal information," he began. "It is up to you, whether you wish others to know."

The empowerment brought to her by his words made her hold her head up. "You may tell us all, Doctor," she said formally.

"Very well. First, you are free of disease. Second, you have minute traces of several statins in your body.

These are medications capable of affecting and suppressing your memories, and leaving you vulnerable to replacement memories. The rush of memories you've just experienced is due to the weakness of those traces, and I suspect the last time the statins were administered was as long ago as ten days. You may find more memories filtering in from time to time."

"How would these statins have been administered," Kamie asked.

Lawal's lips tightened as he considered. "As you, Janesha, were not aware of it, having taken no pills, I'd say they were put into a beverage. Nothing strong or acidic, as these would have reduced their effects." He glanced at the empty mug on the table. "Certainly not coffee. Tea, perhaps."

"He wouldn't let me have coffee," she said irritably. "It was always tea, tea, tea."

"Who wouldn't, Janesha?" Kamie asked quickly, while the memory was still fresh.

"The majordomo," she replied. "Snarrel Goodling."

"But I think he has help," Hallia put in. "Recently he's had a couple meetings with Clewthe Neerdawell, the majordomo of Lascora Castle."

"Neerdawell," mused Lawal. "I know that name...he did a monograph on toxicology...this was years ago, let me see...twelve years ago, as I recall. It was quite good."

"Goodling is going to poison them," Kamie said dully. "And I don't know how we can stop him." A moment later she added, to Janesha, "It's not you."

"What's not me?"

"Last night I said that something was missing from what we knew and what we were doing," she explained. "Something we needed to know, or maybe something that had to happen. For a while here I thought it might be you, Janesha. But no...it's something else. If it's there at all."

A brief silence followed, broken by Lawal. "As regards your identity, Janesha, you are in fact the daughter of the Duchess Palologa. But the duke is not your father. That would be one Verron Ecke, a purveyor of dinnerware, who died five years ago. I'm sorry."

"We have to do *something*," said Jinzy.

"And we have early work to do," said Garla, as she headed for the kitchen. She made a little gesture toward the door, where an airfoil had just docked behind Lawal's. "Early patrons want breakfast."

There were three of them: one man—tall, with dark hair and sharp blue eyes; one brown woman almost his height; and one woman with flame-orange hair. It was this last who took one look at Janesha and breathed, "Goddesses."

An agitated clamor ensued, centered on the physical similarities between Hoya and Janesha. There was mutual recognition among almost everyone save March and Myrrha, who were reduced to looking on in wonder and speculating as to relationships and identities.

Garla allowed the tumult to go on for several minutes. After several sharp reports from her clapping hands got everyone's attention, she said, "It's too early for ale, so let's all have coffee, tea, or juice. In the meantime, I'm not sure about those two," here she indicated March and Myrrha, "but everyone else here is acquainted in one way or another. Jinzy, Hallia, I could use some help with the beverages." She pointed at March. "There's a Closed sign hanging from a hook there in the corner. If you would hang it on the door, so we may forestall interruptions while we sort this out."

Calm thus restored, March and Kamie and Hoya joined two tables. Seating was uncertain at first, until Myrrha took over that task, placing Hoya opposite Catalina/Janesha, herself facing March, and Jinzy and Hallia confronting Garla and Kamie. Although the arrangement was sensible, questions whirled about them like a storm trying to gather itself. Myrrha was not acquainted with Kamie or Jinzy. Following very brief, almost terse introductions, she brought the conference directly to the point.

"I think March and I have learned enough to determine who most of us are and what our stories are," she said, and proceeded to summarize, with a few nudges of correction from the others, where needed, particularly regarding the dinner.

When she was finished, Kamie said, "So how do we stop the assassination without getting Duke Justinio killed? Because the majordomo is not going to take interference well, and if this is the crucial moment, he may be armed to ensure success if necessary."

"I was thinking about that on the way here," said Myrrha. "The dinner setting was the last piece of the puzzle."

"You have a plan?" March asked her.

She nodded. "I just need to know where the guards with halberds will be standing, because they'll have to be neutralized."

"They'll stand on either side of the main door, just inside the dining hall," said Janesha. "But please don't kill them."

March shook his head. "They're innocent bystanders. They'll be protected. Myrrha?"

She exhaled a deep breath and looked to Hallia. "Here's what you do," she began...

# 022: Plan and Execution

Gusts of wind swirled the gardener's long, straw-yellow hair this way and that as she applied the snippers to some unruly branches of a tremblewhite bush that grew against the back wall of Palologa Castle. Attired in work garb almost as white as the bush's six-petaled flowers, she hurried along. Above, the sky was morose and sullen here and blue there, almost as if it were debating whether to storm or clear, and she was unwilling to wait by idly while it decided.

She was about to move on to another shrub, this one a doveling and one of the duchess's favorites, when she heard and then felt a light burst of air coming from the direction of the shagbark grove some two hundred paces away, and turned to see what had caused it. An electric blue egg had deTracked and downdocked on the other side of the grove, and someone was disembarking from it. Puzzled, she watched as a young woman made her way around the trees and headed for her. The egg then vanished, and the woman paid no attention to it. As she drew closer, the gardener recognized her. Hallia had returned from wherever she had run off to.

Several branches of the doveling bore well-faded gray-violet flowers, and the gardener turned back to deadhead them. Moments later, her spine stiffened, and she knew that Hallia had come to stand behind her.

"Desshelle," whispered Hallia.

"I did not expect you to come back," said the gardener, her tone neutral although she was relieved to see Hallia again. She turned to face her. "You should go. Goodling is...I fear for Cinya. If he should spot you..."

Hallia's eyes rejected this advice. She made a little gesture toward the back door. "Is anyone about in there?"

"Just Cinya, in the kitchen. Most everyone is taking time off, with the duke and duchess off on a walkabout." Desshelle's green eyes narrowed, for the sun had just burst through the clouds. "Is something wrong?"

Hallia hesitated. "I have to get inside and not be seen. Where is the majordomo?"

"Fretting, I think, in his office."

"That's good."

"Hallia, what are you...wait, never mind. Don't tell me. If I don't know, it wasn't I who told."

Hallia reached out to Desshelle's arm, and gently squeezed it. "Thank you."

"And I suppose I haven't seen you. Hallia...be careful. If Goodling sees you, he'll go spare."

Desshelle watched as Hallia cautiously opened the back door and slipped inside. A glance up told her that the storm was clearing. Perhaps that bode well for whatever Hallia was doing. She hoped it had something to do with the majordomo.

\* \* \*

Snarrel Goodling was mildly surprised when Catalina showed up for the dinner with her parents. He had been told, or led to believe, that she was still on flyabout, exploring the countryside. Her presence was problematic only in that she would watch her father die at the table, and her reaction was impossible to predict. Still, once the duke was dead, that reaction was irrelevant.

He stood waiting now at the foot of the great stonewood table, while Justinio and Olena took their time approaching the head. Cinya had done excellent work with the arrangements—the napkins and silverware just so, the spaces properly measured to accommodate the plates she would bring out, the tablecloth placed so that it exposed some areas of varnished dark wood and yet protected that wood from spills, should they occur. Faintly-lit chandeliers dribbled light throughout the room, and this was augmented by candles before each place setting. In the flickering light, the silk raiment of the duke and duchess fairly glistened—he with dark trousers and pale yellow tunic, she in a long floral dining gown made to be worn only once, then handed off.

Goodling stood, because no one might sit down until the duke and duchess had seated themselves. While he waited, he counted the place settings. Two for the ducal couple, one for himself, one for Catalina, and one for...

He almost gasped at Desshelle, standing behind a chair as if she meant to sit in it. The duke was eating *with the help*? He fought to keep the "unheard-of" expression from his face as he calmed himself. This might be new policy, but it would be short-lived. Rules would be restored after he took over. He filed a mental note to have the groundskeeping quiff eat outdoors with her precious stinking roses.

He made fists to keep from fidgeting. What was taking so long?

Olena had locked up Justinio's arm in hers, and it was impossible to determine who was leading whom. At length the duke freed himself and pulled the chair out for her, waiting while she adjusted her gown before helping her ease forward to her place setting. With a slow gaze around the dining hall, a sweep that included nods at the two guards with halberds standing at the main door, Justinio seated himself. After taking a moment to settle in, and to cast benevolent smiles at each at the table in turn, he clapped his hands twice.

From the kitchen doorway emerged Cinya, pushing a small cart that bore five bowls of soup. Steam wafted upwards from each bowl as she placed them before those who were about to dine. Finished, she returned the cart to the kitchen to receive the next course. Meanwhile, Justinio diddled with his spoon, as if he were unaware that none at the table could begin on the soup until he took a spoonful. Finally he dipped into the bowl and supped at the spoon—the soup was hot, but did not appear to bother him. The dinner began.

Small salads, delivered again by Cinya, followed the soup. As she cleared away the soup bowls and spoons, Goodling noticed a bit of tension in her expression, but dared not draw attention to her with a remark. All she had to do was follow instructions. All the duke had to do was take a few bites of trake. All he, Goodling, had to do was prepare himself to rule.

Belatedly he noticed that Catalina was engaged in quiet intermittent conversation with her father. At one point she shook her head, in apparent response to a question from him. At this, the duke scowled briefly. Goodling wished he could hear the words.

Suddenly he could hear them, for she had raised her voice. "No," she said. "I'm going to renounce it."

That stunned Goodling. If she meant to abdicate her throne after the duke's demise, then he, Goodling, might achieve power even earlier than he had planned. Anticipation cheered and galvanized him. Where the ruddy blazes was that trake?

Take a deep breath. Calm yourself. Everything is going according to plan. Just a couple of very minor glitches, nothing more than that. Five bites, maybe a few more, and it's all over. There was no antidote, only a countermeasure which had only the smallest chance of success. Neerdawell ruddy well better be right about that, for it was imperative that Justinio die here and now.

Just a few more minutes. You can hold your breath that long.

Two trays of freshly-baked rolls, one at each end of the table, arrived next, along with round plates of ornate blue and white porcelain bearing slabs of suitably softened butter. The aroma of the warm rolls soon permeated the area around the table. Justinio and Olena drew breaths of it, while Goodling sniffed disdainfully; bread was, after all, bread. He watched while Desshelle sliced open her roll, filled the little crevasse with butter, and gnawed at it.

At least, he thought, she had not slurped her soup, and had kept her mouth closed while chewing her salad.

*Eating with the help. Disgusting.* But he did not say this aloud.

*The trake. Where's the trake? Bring the trake.* Under the table, he made hard fists, his nails biting into his palms.

As if reading his mind, Cinya rolled the cart out again, this time laden with plates and small bowls. Each plate bore a slab of pale yellow, deboned fish freckled with herbs and adorned with sprigs of parsley. Each bowl contained a serving of boiled green vegetables. Goodling's eyes widened, and his frown deepened. Cinya was headed *his way*?

*No, you stupid quiff. You serve the duke first!*

He could almost hear the beads of sweat bursting onto his forehead. He dared not wipe at them and thereby draw attention to his alarmed state.

But at the last moment, Cinya turned the cart and made for the duke's place setting. Goodling heard her say, "For you, Your Grace," as she set the plate before him. The majordomo found himself wishing he might have said that, not her. Not that it mattered.

Plates and bowls distributed, Cinya returned the cart to the kitchen, and came back to take her place behind Justinio to await his orders. She caught Goodling's eye and gave him the tiniest nod. He breathed a little sigh of relief.

Duke Justinio did not hesitate, but cut free a piece of the fillet and crammed it into his mouth. This signaled permission to everyone else at the table to do the same. Goodling now eased a longer sigh. As always, the trake was tender, flaky, and utterly delicious. Nobody spoke; all were focused on the main course.

A few more minutes for the toxin to take effect. Goodling dared not look at the duke. After several bites of trake, he reached for another roll, biding his time.

Catalina smiled at her mother. The majordomo wondered what was going on with her. The groundskeeper, Desshelle, was engrossed with her own fillet, as if she had never before partaken of such a repast.

*Any moment now.*

The roll seemed a bit dry and tasteless. Anticipation began to dominate his senses. A decade and more of scheming, manipulation, and deceit was about to reach fruition.

The duke stopped chewing. This is it, thought Goodling, fumbling with his roll.

*Calm yourself. You can't show any sign of...*

The duke cleared his throat, as if about to speak. Words seemed to fail him. Goodling sat on tenterhooks. He almost revealed his agitation by inadvertently striking his nose with the roll. *Careful, you fool. Get it into your mouth.* The duke's lips moved, but he emitted no sound. But he seemed to be looking at Cinya. Was that accusation on his face? Goodling couldn't tell from his angle of vision. He did not expect the duke to utter a word now. Matters had gone past that. But he couldn't resist.

"How is the trake, sire?" he asked solicitously. A frown overtook him; his voice sounded odd.

Justinio responded clearly, but to Cinya. "The poached trake is excellent. My compliments to the cook."

A figure emerged from the shadows inside the kitchen doorway. Hallia stood in the light and looked directly at Goodling, "That would be me," she said.

Panic exploded through Goodling. His mind filled with too many thoughts at once. He was lucid, but his muscles were beginning to decline his commands. Now, too late, he understood why the roll had tasted dry, why he had missed his mouth with it, why his words had slightly malformed. Still, he retained some capacity for movement. What was it Neerdawell had told him? Yes, drink lots of water to dilute the toxin, then vomit. Do it quickly. He reached for his glass of water with a hand starting to tremble...and knocked it over, spilling it all.

"'Oooh!" he yelled in protest, unable to form an N with the tip of his tongue.

Still, he had a chance. If he could just survive. Tetradotoxin was not always lethal, just mostly. He fumbled for the sidearm under his tunic. It took three attempts before he was able to grasp the butt of it.

"What's the matter?" cried the duke, alert now to Goodling.

Catalina steadied Justinio with a hand to his arm.

Finally Goodling tugged his Krupp Narn free. Desshelle shoved the duchess under the table, and ducked down there herself. Goodling had to use both hands to steady his aim. His thumb refused to press the Enable button, so he squeezed his palm against it. In the instant before the weapon fired, Catalina threw herself in front of Justinio. The blue beam took her full in the chest, and she sprawled onto the table with a clattering of ceramics and silverware.

Belatedly, the two guards started toward the majordomo. At that moment, the main door burst open and March rushed into the dining hall, his Sizzler at the ready. Quickly he confronted the guards, who stopped, uncertain whether to bring their halberds into defense against an energy weapon.

"Let this play out," March told them. "The duke is in no danger."

Their hesitation signaled compliance—they were after all present for appearance's sake—but March remained firmly in place, with scarcely a glance over his shoulder.

Goodling's mind remained perfectly lucid as he felt his enfeebled body slipping from his chair and onto the floor. His fingers were unable to maintain their grasp of the Krupp, and it spilled onto the hardwood floor beside him. Hallia stepped forward and kicked it away, toward

March, before coming to hover over the supine majordomo. She spoke not a word as she placidly gazed down at him. Her expression suggested that she was wondering who had made this mess on the floor.

Now Duke Justinio gasped. Entering through the kitchen doorway were Catalina and...and Catalina? Already half-risen from his chair to worry over Catalina on the table, he looked as if his mind had just fractured.

"It's all right, Appa," said one of the two newly-arrived Catalinas.

The Catalina on the table sat up and examined her blouse for scorch marks. Finding none, she slid from the table and stood up.

Seeing this, the duke, now fully on his feet, tottered, dizzy with shock. His mouth worked as he tried to form a question. Finally he managed a, "What?" and got no further. His gray eyes rounded as the Catalina before him transformed into a taller and brown young woman in a short, pale blue tunic and yellow-brown leather boots up to the thighs. With two hands she steadied him.

"If Your Grace pleases," Myrrha said, with disarming courtesy. "Sit down, and we'll explain." She turned her head and called, "Duchess Olena, it is safe to come out from under there. Desshelle, if you would see her back to her chair?"

"Who...?" said the duke, accepting Myrrha's nudge.

Goodling was unable to feel anything. None of his flesh responded to his will, to his commands. But his mind remained clear and aware as he peered up at Hallia, who had yet to say a word to him. She seemed to be waiting for something; he knew what it was. Helpless frustration set in. She was just a kitchen quiff. Who was she to...to...?

He could scarcely draw air into his lungs now, or expel it. His eyelids refused to blink, and his eyes dried. Strangely, he felt no pain but that of utter failure. He thought that, given the choice, he would have greatly preferred the physical pain. Even as darkness poised to strike, and despite his will to evade it, he was aware that he had drawn his last breath. As he wondered whether he would exhale, the forever black saved him from the final ignominy of knowing that despite all his power he had entered it utterly limp and helpless.

# 023: Fruition

"So you are a computer?" Justinio asked Myrrha, after March had completed his explanatory narrative.

She smiled warmly. "I am a woman, Your Grace. But...well, it's complicated. Just take it as writ that I can assume form at will. As March said, there was a chance of weapons fire, and you had to be protected. Only I could do that, but to be in position to do it I had to take on a form that would not arouse suspicion, for we had to let Goodling reveal his true nature. The clothes and skin you see are an integral part of me, and for this dinner they are constructed of an impermeable metalloplastic, the same substance as a 'skip's hull." She shrugged. "However, I have just altered them back into fabric and flesh, now that the threat has been eliminated. Much more comfortable. And *these*," she gestured, "are your true daughters."

He turned to Hoya. "And you are my real daughter," he said. "You are the heir to the throne."

"Yes, and no," said Myrrha, before Hoya could speak. "If I may, Your Grace, you have regarded Catalina as your daughter for over a decade now. I'd say that qualifies her for full daughterhood, wouldn't you? But Hoya is the proper heir."

"But I've been a...a neglectful father," said the duke, shaking his head.

"But learning, Appa," Catalina pointed out. "I will always love you and Amma."

"But you have renounced your investment," Justinio reminded her.

"It was not mine to accept, Appa. Hoya should have stood there on the dais."

Frowning, he turned to Hoya. "Yet you lay claim, not to the throne, but to another career."

"In spite of what you might think about that career, Appa, I am doing some good out there. I wish to continue doing it."

"But...but then who will...?"

"I am sure you don't have to ask that for a long time yet, Appa," said Catalina affectionately.

The duke looked at Olena. "But your mother and I, we wanted to travel..."

"What's stopping you, Appa?" said Hoya.

"But...but...oh, bother." He turned to Hallia and Cinya. "My dears, I owe you a great debt of gratitude for saving my life."

Both dipped curtseys. "It was my honor, sire," said Hallia. She toed the totally slack body of the majordomo. "If I might suggest, sire, someone should dispose of this. It's already beginning to smell."

Justinio continued to worry. "Someone has to be here while we are away," he said. "The throne should not be vacant."

Myrrha tokked her Palmetto and spoke softly into it. A few moments later, Kamie Isaora entered through the still-open main doorway, attired in a fresh outsuit as pink as some of the roses outside.

"Now who are you?" asked Justinio. "Wait: don't you work in the Isaora kitchen?"

"I used to, Appa."

"Appa?" he said sourly. "I think you forget your place, young lady."

"I was born twenty-seven years ago in this castle," Kamie said softly, but respectfully. "DNA makes you my father. My age makes me the eldest daughter, and the heir to the throne in the absence of male issue and in view of Hoya's abdication. My mother is Garla Korkyam."

His face, especially his eyes, declared that he remembered Garla, and his expression softened. He risked a glance at Olena, who promptly laid an "It's all right, my liege" hand on his arm. Still, he found a mild protest. "But...but you are not trained..."

"Not formally, Appa, no. But as Amma—my mother—told me earlier today, when we were planning all this, I have had better informal schooling in life itself. I have worked in scullery and on the grounds, alongside others who find silvers and bronzes difficult to come by. The hours have been long and arduous, and frequently irritating. My lesson is this: scullery must be done; dusting and cleaning must be done; shrubs must be trimmed or pruned." Here she threw in a grin. "Croquet lawns must be kept low. But these necessary tasks and others need not be made miserable or oppressive by overseers. Appa, for two days now I have been working as a food and beverage server in a tavern in Carrikdove known as *The Parsley Sprig*. I wanted to continue working there; I had no wish to be a princess. As I told Amma, when she learned what we were going to do, there is nothing wrong with tavern work. To this, she said, 'Go. Just go. You have a chance to do something with your life. You can make a difference in the lives of the people of Palologa, in others as well, by your example and attitude.' Me, I think she overestimates me. I am and have been a simple peasant girl. But I am also," and here she stood up even straighter; she was almost his height, "I am also your daughter. In the wake of the abdication and the renunciation, I become the heir-apparent...if you will have me."

Justinio turned to Olena. "It looks as if we're going traveling after all, my dear."

Kamie looked to Desshelle. "I'm going to need a majordomo," she said.

After the gardener's mouth closed back, she asked, "M-may I still continue to tend my plants, Milady?"

"I would not have it any other way."

"I would," said March. "I'm thirsty. I suggest we all adjourn to *The Parsley Sprig* and do something about the overabundance of ale on this world."

# Epilogue

The evening crowd at *The Parsley Sprig* had already dissipated by the time the ducal party arrived. Only Caber, sitting quietly at a table with Jinzy, remained. Garla stopped her nightly cleanup to draw ales and restart the grill, pleased but not greatly surprised by this particular influx of patrons. Jinzy and Hallia moved to assist her; she started to wave them off, but after taking headcount she changed her mind.

Despite the utter success of Myrrha's plan, the overall mood was subdued, and only a little festive. No cheer accompanied their few words as March and Myrrha brought two tables together. Justinio and Olena, though cordially welcome in the tavern, looked as though they felt out of place at first. Gradually, however, they settled in, and drank appreciatively of the ale when it was delivered to them. Talk accompanied the drinking, but it was of that nature that no one would recall afterwards. Bits and fragments floated past one another on the way to the person to whom they were addressed, and sometimes they went astray. It did not matter.

All the while, Caber spoke little and listened much. He had the demeanor of one who was becoming acquainted with a family he had never known existed. Jinzy had the look of one who was learning very quickly that some men were worth it—one in particular. It was obvious to anyone who looked at them that under the table they were holding hands.

Eventually the atmosphere shifted to somber relief. If it hadn't been for Hallia. If it hadn't been for Cinya. Had it not been for Myrrha. Had March and Myrrha evaded answering a distress signal. Had-nots and ifs abounded.

Then there were the subtle things. Kamie rescuing Jinzy and Hallia. Hoya trying to reach Hallia. Kamie not closing out the Palmetto outright in disbelief of Hoya's claim. So much might have gone wrong.

"Another ale, Your Grace?" asked Jinzy.

Justinio gave her a mock sour frown. "In this tavern," he replied, with a hint of light humor, "I believe I would prefer something rather in between 'Your Grace' and...and..."

"Oy, Matey?" tried Myrrha.

After the laughter subsided, Jinzy asked, "Another ale, sire?"

"Please."

Garla brought it. Following delivery, she paused, as if she wanted to do something more. After a long look at her, Olena edged against the duke to create an unoccupied spot on the bench next to her. No further communication on that topic was needed between the two women.

*The* question finally came, and it from Hallia. "What happens now?" she wanted to know.

Everyone looked to Kamie, who said firmly, "I will not be Duchess for a good century and more," she reminded them.

"But you will be invested," Justinio pointed out. "That title conveys the duke's authority in his absence."

She tried a feeble protest. "But I've only made a few decisions regarding what I want to happen."

The duke lifted his mug to her. "So make a few more."

"Appa," she sighed, with mild exasperation, and took a gulp of ale. "So all right. Let's find out who I have to work with. Who wants to be where? After that, we may want to consider rooms upstairs; I'm starting to feel some of this ale."

\* \* \*

"In the end," said March, sitting in the starboard captain's chair on the bridge of the *Bluebolt*, "for all our wanting to help, we really didn't do that much except be in the right place at the right time."

In the port chair Myrrha shrugged. "Kismet." A moment later, she said, "You sound disappointed. All's well that ends well; this ended well. Hallia is staying on at the tavern. Jinzy is definitely staying on at the tavern."

"Because of Caber."

"Just so. And you giving Garla a thousand silvers to hold in the event they do work out—which I think they will—that will get them off to a good start. Cinya takes over the kitchen. Desshelle is majordomo." Here she laughed. "Or minordomo, as she put it, until she learns the position. Satrin Hommer has to find work elsewhere, if he can. I doubt he will have the Palologa endorsement. The duke and duchess will travel on Faedra and then elsewhere, and he said something about building a Faedra historical museum, not a bad idea."

"Hoya is going to pay Clewthe Neerdawell one of her 'special' visits, no charge," mused March. "Janesha is bound tomorrow for Margent and pre-university studies."

"She's very intelligent, and determined now. She'll make up the learning she didn't receive, and the university will take her. I'd give it three years until she graduates." Myrrha gave a light, almost distracted laugh. "A mind like hers, still almost a blank slate. I wonder what she'll become."

"None of which we had anything to do with," he pointed out.

"We were the catalyst," she countered. "Sometimes that's enough. It is rare for us to know the effects we have on others, *mon amour*. As for what's next, I love your idea of traveling around, getting involved where we can help. Who knows, maybe one day Janesha will join us; she likes to travel, and she has a good heart."

"Um..."

"Why not? I said you could have other women."

March shook his head. His lips puffed out as he exhaled. "I can barely cope with one."

A light and comfortable silence settled in. The effects of the ale still on him, he gazed with unfocused eyes at the matte black of null-space in the Videx. In altering the lives of others, he had also redirected his own. He was coming to find that remarkable, and most agreeable.

Finally Myrrha broke into his reverie. "Course heading?"

"Stateroom."

She chuckled. "I meant, for the 'skip."

"Ravensworld. There's a bazaar open in a few hours. I want to buy a necklace."